THE HUMAN CHORD

THE HUMAN CHORD

ALGERNON BLACKWOOD

With an introduction by
MIKE ASHLEY

This edition first published in 2024 by
The British Library
96 Euston Road
London NW1 2DB

The Human Chord was first published in 1910 by Macmillan and Co., Ltd, London.

Introduction © 2024 Mike Ashley
Volume copyright © 2024 The British Library Board

Cataloguing in Publication Data
A catalogue record for this publication is available from the British Library

ISBN 978 0 7123 5441 4
e-ISBN 978 0 7123 6877 3

Cover and frontispiece design by Mauricio Villamayor
with illustration by Mag Ruhig
Chapter openers by Emmeline Richardson, reproduced
from the first edition of *The Human Chord*
Text design and typesetting by Tetragon, London
Printed in England by CPI Group (UK) Ltd, Croydon, CR0 4YY

CONTENTS

Introduction   7

A Note from the Publisher   13

THE HUMAN CHORD

Chapter I	19
Chapter II	46
Chapter III	69
Chapter IV	85
Chapter V	96
Chapter VI	104
Chapter VII	109
Chapter VIII	120
Chapter IX	131
Chapter X	145
Chapter XI	160
Chapter XII	171
Chapter XIII	180
Chapter XIV	197

INTRODUCTION

I suspect we've all heard of the belief that if an opera singer's voice can reach the right frequency, they can shatter a wine glass. It's not easy, but it is possible as the TV series *Mythbusters* proved back in 2005.

It's all a matter of vibration and the concept of vibration fascinated one of the great writers of supernatural fiction, Algernon Blackwood (1869–1951). It permeates much of his work. In perhaps his best-known story, "The Willows" (1907), two travellers on a remote island in the river Danube experience a strange humming sound, like "an immense gong, suspended far up in the sky", which creates funnels in the sand. One of the travellers believes that the sound creates a vortex between our three-dimensional world and that of a fourth dimension, normally separated from us by vibrations.

Blackwood discussed it in more detail in a lesser-known story, "A Victim of Higher Space", featuring his psychic detective John Silence, written in 1907. Blackwood used the phrase "Higher Space" to describe the fourth dimension, a dimension which is all around us but of which normally we are unaware. However, as he explains:

"Certain people, certain human atmospheres, certain wandering forces, thoughts, desires even—the radiations of certain combinations of colour, and above all, the vibrations of certain kinds of music, will suddenly throw me into a state of what I can only describe as an intense and terrific inner vibration—and behold I am off! Off in the direction at right angles to all our known directions! Off in the direction the cube takes when it begins to trace the outlines of the new figure! Off into my breathless and semi-divine Higher Space! Off, inside myself, into the world of four dimensions!"

Blackwood was aware of the power of vibrations from an early age. He had learned to play the violin in his youth and it is easy to show how playing a single note on a violin string will set up vibrations and create patterns in sand spread across a table or tray. But his detailed knowledge of the power of sound emerged when, in October 1900, he joined the occult organization the Hermetic Order of the Golden Dawn. Blackwood was intrigued by the nature and purpose of the world, what controlled its forces and whether humans could control any of those forces. He had been born into a highly religious family with strong Calvinist beliefs and had been brought up in an atmosphere of rigid Christian discipline. Any transgression from the strict Christian code meant that his soul was doomed. This proved too much for the young Blackwood who believed there was much more to human ethics and behaviour. He was drawn to Eastern wisdom, especially Buddhism, which satiated his growing fascination for the natural world, and from that to theosophy. This was a belief system promoted by the Russian-born mystic Helena Blavatsky who established the Theosophical Society in New York in 1875. Theosophy was a blending of beliefs from several Eastern religions coupled with an understanding of older primeval religions. Theosophy suggested greater spiritual freedom, not the restrictions imposed by his parents' beliefs.

The Golden Dawn grew, to some extent, out of theosophy, blending the Eastern beliefs with the western hermetic tradition. Blackwood became totally absorbed in his studies for progression through the Golden Dawn grades and during his first two years he proceeded to the Philosophus Grade, the highest grade in the First Order, but he chose not to progress into the Second Grade and

INTRODUCTION

become an adept, unlike arguably the most notorious member of the Golden Dawn, Aleister Crowley. Blackwood had been introduced to the Golden Dawn by no less than the Irish poet W. B. Yeats and other well known members of the Order included Arthur Machen and A. E. Waite.

Blackwood's studies and his understanding of the Hebrew kabbala began to feature in his stories, notably "With Intent to Steal" and "Smith: An Episode in a Lodging House" (both 1906) but the full force of his studies coalesced in *The Human Chord*. Key to this story is the concept of "words of power". The basic premise is that everything has a "true name", not the name by which we might know it. That true name is usually hidden because if anyone learns it they can have power over that object. Of most importance are the true names of deities and demons, a belief that dates back to the ancient Egyptians and Assyrians and also features in ancient Hebrew beliefs. Of greatest significance is the true name of God, usually represented in Hebrew by the initials YHWH, known as the Tetragrammaton. YHWH is usually pronounced as Yahweh from which comes Jehovah, but the true pronunciation depends on the intonation of the letters, the pitch of the voice, the emphasis of each letter and the overall sound and vibration.

In *The Human Chord* we meet Philip Skale, a retired clergyman who believes he knows how to recreate the true pronunciation of YHWH. He has already captured certain sounds which he keeps in jars for use at the final invocation, but he also needs to recruit three other individuals besides himself who have perfect pitch as tenor, soprano and alto—Skale provides the base. These four are the eponymous "human chord". As the novel progresses, we witness the power that Skale can invoke through sound and vibration including turning himself invisible. The novel builds with inevitable power until the moment of the fateful invocation.

The story is told with passion and conviction as only someone with a detailed knowledge of the subject can achieve and it ranks as one of Blackwood's best novels. It received positive reviews when it was published in October 1910. Hilaire Belloc proclaimed it as being "as powerful as can be" and that it should be "a matter of national pride".

One may wonder, did Blackwood base any of the characters upon real people, in particular Philip Skale. He is described as a "huge figure of a man" with a "floating grey beard". That description fits, to some degree, William Westcott (1848–1925), one of the founders of the Golden Dawn, who also had a booming bass voice. But Westcott had less to do with the Golden Dawn by the time Blackwood joined as it was undergoing a period of disruption amongst its membership resulting in a split creating a successor organization, the Stella Matutina, of which Westcott remained a member, whilst Blackwood remained with the reconstituted Golden Dawn under A. E. Waite. A more likely candidate is William Ayton (1816–1909) who was indeed a retired clergyman with an interest in invocation. The fact that he had died just as Blackwood was writing *The Human Chord* suggests that Blackwood felt more at liberty to use his character. There is one other possible candidate and that is Aleister Crowley himself, not because of any similarity in build or character but because Crowley was known to have invoked spirits in an episode that Blackwood used as the basis for his story "Smith: An Episode in a Lodging House" (reprinted in the British Library volume *The Whisperers*). Crowley was never close to Blackwood and was dismissive of *The Human Chord*, not wishing to encourage any comparisons. It is likely, then, that Skale is a composite using Westcott's voice and physique, Ayton's knowledge and background and perhaps Crowley's abilities.

There was clearly no love lost between Crowley and Blackwood and he took the opportunity in reviewing *The Human Chord* to suggest it was an imitation of *No. 19* by Edgar Jepson, even though

Blackwood had already completed *The Human Chord* and despatched it to his publisher, Macmillan, before *No. 19* was published in March 1910. It concerns a black magician who seeks to invoke demons of the Abyss and in particular the spirit of the god Pan, but there is no reference to words of power, or Hebrew magic. I suspect Blackwood knew Jepson—Jepson knew most literary folk in the early twentieth century and was a close friend of Arthur Machen's—so it's possible Jepson and Blackwood discussed their respective interests, but to imply Blackwood had consciously copied Jepson is absurd. Perhaps it was something in the air, because at the same time M. R. James was recounting the story "Casting the Runes" to his students which involves a curse that the occultist Karswell passes on to those he wishes to die. The curse is in the form of runes which are themselves "words of power" even though they are written and not spoken. It has been argued that Karswell is another literary incarnation of Crowley.

The idea of knowing the true name of someone or something is ancient. It occurs in the *Odyssey*, where Odysseus hides his real name from Polyphemus only to declare it later with dire consequences. In the folk tale "Rumpelstiltskin", best remembered in the version retold by the Brothers Grimm, the mischievous imp lays a claim on a firstborn child unless the mother can discover the imp's name. More recently, readers of the Earthsea trilogy by Ursula K. Le Guin, which began in 1968 with *A Wizard of Earthsea*, will recall that central to the plot is the fact that the young mage, Sparrowhawk, is menaced by a shadow creature that he released and must seeks its true name to control it. The whole concept of God's true name was lampooned to a degree in Arthur C. Clarke's "The Nine Billion Names of God" (1953) where a computer is used to identify all the possible names and, when that is achieved, it brings an end to all things.

The knowledge and practise of the occult goes far back in fiction but in more recent years became best presented in *Zanoni* (1842) by

Lord Bulwer-Lytton. The eponymous mage uses magic to his own advantage but in the process unleashes the powerful Guardian of the Threshold, which can exercise power over Zanoni.

The Human Chord, though, was the first novel to bring together the concept of the true name within a novel involving words of power and ceremonial magic. It remains a significant novel in its own right or, in the words of Hilaire Belloc, "a matter of national pride". It's time we remembered its own true name!

MIKE ASHLEY, 2024

Mike Ashley is an award-winning author, anthologist and genre encyclopaedia editor with a specialism for seeking out rare stories from the periodicals and magazines of the nineteenth and twentieth centuries. He has edited multiple collections of lost stories for the Tales of the Weird series—including *Queens of the Abyss*, *From the Depths*, *Glimpses of the Unknown* and *The Ghost Slayers*—along with hardback volumes of stories by Algernon Blackwood, Arthur Conan Doyle and Margaret Oliphant.

A NOTE FROM THE PUBLISHER

The original short stories reprinted in the British Library Tales of the Weird series were written and published in a period ranging across the nineteenth and twentieth centuries. There are many elements of these stories which continue to entertain modern readers; however, in some cases there are also uses of language, instances of stereotyping and some attitudes expressed by narrators or characters which may not be endorsed by the publishing standards of today. We acknowledge therefore that some elements in the stories selected for reprinting may continue to make uncomfortable reading for some of our audience. With this series British Library Publishing aims to offer a new readership a chance to read some of the rare material of the British Library's collections in an affordable paperback format, to enjoy their merits and to look back into the worlds of the past two centuries as portrayed by their writers. It is not possible to separate these stories from the history of their writing and as such the following novel is presented as it was originally published with minor edits only, made for consistency of style and sense. We welcome feedback from our readers, which can be sent to the following address:

> British Library Publishing
> The British Library
> 96 Euston Road
> London, NW1 2DB
> United Kingdom

THE HUMAN CHORD

To those who hear.

I

As a boy he constructed so vividly in imagination that he came to believe in the living reality of his creations: for everybody and everything he found names—real names. Inside him somewhere stretched immense playgrounds, compared to which the hay-fields and lawns of his father's estate seemed trivial: plains without horizon, seas deep enough to float the planets like corks, and "such tremendous forests" with "trees like tall pointed hilltops." He had only to close his eyes, drop his thoughts inwards, sink after them himself, call aloud and—see.

His imagination conceived and bore—worlds; but nothing in these worlds became alive until he discovered its true and living name. The name was the breath of life; and, sooner or later, he invariably found it.

Once, having terrified his sister by affirming that a little man he had created would come through her window at night and weave a peaked cap for himself by pulling out all her hairs "that hadn't gone to sleep with the rest of her body," he took characteristic measures to protect her from the said depredations. He sat up the entire night on the lawn beneath her window to watch, believing firmly that what his imagination had made alive would come to pass.

She did not know this. On the contrary, he told her that the little man had died suddenly; only, he sat up to make sure. And, for a boy of eight, those cold and haunted hours must have seemed endless from ten o'clock to four in the morning, when he crept back to his own corner of the night nursery. He possessed, you see, courage as well as faith and imagination.

Yet the name of the little man was nothing more formidable than "Winky!"

"You might have known he wouldn't hurt you, Teresa," he said. "Any one with that name would be light as a fly and awf'ly gentle—a regular dicky sort of chap!"

"But he'd have pincers," she protested, "or he couldn't pull the hairs out. Like an earwig he'd be. Ugh!"

"Not Winky! Never!" he explained scornfully, jealous of his offspring's reputation. "He'd do it with his rummy little fingers."

"Then his fingers would have claws at the ends!" she insisted; for no amount of explanation could persuade her that a person named Winky could be nice and gentle, even though he were "quicker than a second." She added that his death rejoiced her.

"But I can easily make another—such a nippy little beggar, and twice as hoppy as the first. Only I won't do it," he added magnanimously, "because it frightens you."

For to name with him was to create. He had only to run out some distance into his big mental prairie, call aloud a name in a certain commanding way, and instantly its owner would run up to claim it. Names described souls. To learn the name of a thing or person was to know all about them and make them subservient to his will; and "Winky" could only have been a very soft and furry little person, swift as a shadow, nimble as a mouse—just the sort of fellow who *would* make a conical cap out of a girl's fluffy hair... and love the mischief of doing it.

And so with all things: names were vital and important. To address beings by their intimate first names, beings of the opposite sex especially, was a miniature sacrament; and the story of that premature audacity of Elsa with Lohengrin never failed to touch his sense of awe. "What's in a name?" for him, was a significant question—a question of life or death. For to mispronounce a name was a bad blunder, but to name it wrongly was to miss it altogether. Such a thing had no real life, or at best a vitality that would soon fade. Adam knew that! And he pondered much in his childhood over the difficulty Adam must have had "discovering" the correct appellations for some of the queerer animals...

As he grew older, of course, all this faded a good deal, but he never quite lost the sense of reality in names—the significance of a true name, the absurdity of a false one, the cruelty of mispronunciation. One day in the far future, he knew, some wonderful girl would come into his life, singing her own true name like music, her whole personality expressing it just as her lips framed the consonants and vowels—and he would love her. His own name, ridiculous and hateful though it was, would sing in reply. They would be in harmony together in the literal sense, as necessary to one another as two notes in the same chord...

So he also possessed the mystical vision of the poet. What he lacked—such temperaments always do—was the sense of proportion and the careful balance that adjusts cause and effect. And this it is, no doubt, that makes his adventures such "hard sayings." It becomes difficult to disentangle what actually did happen from what conceivably might have happened; what he thinks he saw from what positively *was*.

His early life—to the disgust of his Father, a poor country squire—was a distressing failure. He missed all examinations, muddled all chances, and finally, with £50 a year of his own, and no one to care much what happened to him, settled in London and took any odd job of a secretarial nature that offered itself. He kept to nothing for long, being easily dissatisfied, and ever on the look out for the "job" that might conceal the kind of adventure he wanted. Once the work of the moment proved barren of this possibility, he wearied of it and sought another. And the search seemed prolonged and hopeless, for the adventure he sought was not a common kind, but something that should provide him with a means of escape from a vulgar and noisy world that bored him very much indeed. He sought an adventure that should announce to him a new heaven and a new earth; something that should confirm, if not actually replace, that inner region of wonder and delight he revelled in as a boy, but which education and conflict with a prosaic age had swept away from his nearer consciousness. He sought, that is, an authoritative adventure of the soul.

To look at, one could have believed that until the age of twenty-five he had been nameless, and that a committee had then sat upon the subject and selected the sound best suited to describe him: Spinrobin—Robert. For, had he never seen himself, but run into that inner prairie of his and called aloud "Robert Spinrobin," an individual exactly resembling him would surely have pattered up to claim the name.

He was slight, graceful, quick on his feet and generally alert; took little steps that were almost hopping, and when he was in a hurry gave him the appearance of "spinning" down the pavement or up the stairs; always wore clothes of some fluffy material, with a low collar and bright red tie; had soft pink cheeks, dancing grey eyes and loosely scattered hair, prematurely thin and unquestionably like feathers. His hands and feet were small and nimble. When he stood in his favourite attitude with hands plunged deep in his pockets, coat-tails slightly spread and flapping, head on one side and hair disordered, talking in that high, twittering, yet very agreeable voice of his, it was impossible to avoid the conclusion that here was—well—Spinrobin, Bobby Spinrobin, "on the job."

For he took on any "job" that promised adventure of the kind he sought, and the queerer the better. As soon as he found that his present occupation led to nothing, he looked about for something new—chiefly in the newspaper advertisements. Numbers of strange people advertised in the newspapers, he knew, just as numbers of strange people wrote letters to them; and Spinny—so he was called by those who loved him—was a diligent student of the columns known as "Agony" and "Help wanted." Whereupon it came about that he was aged twenty-eight, and out of a job, when the threads of the following occurrence wove into the pattern of his life, and "led to something" of a kind that may well be cause for question and amazement.

The advertisement that formed the bait read as follows:—

"WANTED, by Retired Clergyman, Secretarial Assistant with courage and imagination. Tenor voice and some knowledge of Hebrew essential; single; *unworldly*. Apply Philip Skale,"—and the address.

Spinrobin swallowed the bait whole. "Unworldly" put the match, and he flamed up. He possessed, it seemed, the other necessary qualifications; for a thin tenor voice, not unmusical, was his, and also a smattering of Hebrew which he had picked up at Cambridge because he liked the fine, high-sounding names of deities and angels to be found in that language. Courage and imagination he lumped in, so to speak, with the rest, and in the gilt-edged diary he affected he wrote: "Have taken on Skale's odd advertisement. I like the man's name. The experience may prove an adventure. While there's change, there's hope." For he was very fond of turning proverbs to his own use by altering them, and the said diary was packed with absurd misquotations of a similar kind.

II

A singular correspondence followed, in which the advertiser explained with reserve that he wanted an assistant to aid him in certain experiments in sound, that a particular pitch and quality of voice was necessary (which he could not decide until, of course, he had heard it), and that the successful applicant must have sufficient courage and imagination to follow a philosophical speculation "wheresoever it may lead," and also be "so far indifferent to worldly success as to consider it of small account compared to spiritual knowledge—especially if such knowledge appeared within reach and involved worldly sacrifices." He further added that a life of loneliness in the country would have to be faced, and that the man who suited him and worked faithfully should find compensation by inheriting his own "rather considerable property when the time came." For the rest he asked no references and gave none. In a question of spiritual values references were mere foolishness. Each must judge intuitively for himself.

Spinrobin, as has been said, bit. The letters, written in a fine scholarly handwriting, excited his interest extraordinarily. He imagined some dreamer-priest possessed by a singular hobby, searching for things of the spirit by those devious ways he had heard about from time to time, a little mad probably into the bargain. The name Skale sounded to him big, yet he somehow pictured to himself an ascetic-faced man of small stature pursuing in solitude some impossible ideal. It all attracted him hugely with its promise of out-of-the-way adventure. In his own phrase it "might lead to something," and the hints about "experiments in sound" set chords trembling in him that had not vibrated since the days of his boyhood's belief in names and the significance of names. The salary, besides, was good. He was accordingly thrilled and delighted to receive in reply to his last letter a telegram which read: "Engage you month's trial both sides. Take single ticket. Skale."

"I like that 'take single ticket,'" he said to himself as he sped westwards into Wales, dressed in his usual fluffy tweed suit and anarchist tie. Upon his knees lay a brand new Hebrew grammar which he studied diligently all the way to Cardiff, and still carried in his hands when he changed into the local train that carried him laboriously into the desolation of the Pontwaun Mountains. "It looks as though he approved of me already. My name apparently hasn't put him off as it does most people. Perhaps, through it, he divines the real me!"

He smoothed down his rebellious hair as he neared the station in the dusk; but he was surprised to find only a rickety little cart drawn by a donkey sent to meet him (the house being five miles distant in the hills), and still more surprised when a huge figure of a man, hatless, dressed in knickerbockers, and with a large, floating grey beard, strode down the platform as he gave up his ticket to the station-master and announced himself as Mr. Philip Skale. He had expected the small, foxy-faced individual of his imagination, and the shock momentarily deprived him of speech.

"Mr. Spinrobin, of course? I am Mr. Skale—Mr. Philip Skale."

The voice can only be described as booming, it was so deep and vibrating; but the smile of welcome, where it escaped with difficulty from the network of beard and moustaches, was winning and almost gentle in contradistinction to the volume of that authoritative voice. Spinrobin felt slightly bewildered—caught up into a whirlwind that drove too many impressions through his brain for any particular one to be seized and mastered. He found himself shaking hands—Mr. Skale, rather, shaking his, in a capacious grasp as though it were some small indiarubber ball to be squeezed and flung away. Mr. Skale flung it away, he felt the shock up the whole length of his arm to the shoulder. His first impressions, he declares, he cannot remember—they were too tumultuous—beyond that he liked both smile and voice, the former making him feel at home, the latter filling him to the brim with a peculiar sense of well-being. Never before had he heard his name pronounced in quite the same way; it sounded dignified, even splendid, the way Mr. Skale spoke it. Beyond this general impression, however, he can only say that his thoughts and feelings "whirled." Something emanated from this giant clergyman that was somewhat enveloping and took him off his feet. The keynote of the man had been struck at once.

"How do you do, sir? This *is* the train you mentioned, I think?" Spinrobin heard his own thin voice speaking, by way, as it were, of instinctive apology that he should have put such a man to the trouble of coming to meet him. He said "sir," it seemed unavoidable; for there was nothing of the clergyman about him—bishop, perhaps, or archbishop, but no suggestion of vicar or parish priest. Somewhere, too, in his presentment he felt dimly, even at the first, there was an element of the incongruous, a meeting of things not usually found together. The vigorous open-air life of the mountaineer spoke in the great muscular body with the broad shoulders and clean, straight limbs; but behind the brusqueness of manner lay the true gentleness of fine breeding.

And even here, on this platform of the lonely mountain station, Spinrobin detected the atmosphere of the scholar, almost of the recluse, shot through with the strange fires that dropped from the large, lambent, blue eyes. All these things rushed over the thrilled little secretary with an effect, as already described, of a certain bewilderment, that left no single, dominant impression. What remained with him, perhaps, most vividly, he says, was the quality of the big blue eyes, their luminosity, their far-seeing expression, their kindliness. They were the eyes of the true visionary, but in such a personality they proclaimed the mystic who had retained his health of soul and body. Mr. Skale was surely a visionary, but just as surely a wholesome man of action—probably of terrific action. Spinrobin felt irresistibly drawn to him.

"It is not unpleasant, I trust," the other was saying in his deep tones, "to find some one to meet you, and," he added with a genial laugh, "to counteract the first impression of this somewhat melancholy and inhospitable scenery." His arm swept out to indicate the dreary little station and the bleak and lowering landscape of treeless hills in the dusk.

The new secretary made some appropriate reply, his sense of loneliness already dissipated in part by the unexpected welcome. And they fell to arrangements about the luggage. "You won't mind walking," said Mr. Skale, with a finality that anticipated only agreement. "It's a short five miles. The donkey-cart will take the portmanteau." Upon which they started off at a pace that made the little man wonder whether he could possibly keep it up. "We shall get in before dark," explained the other, striding along with ease, "and Mrs. Mawle, my housekeeper, will have tea ready and waiting for us." Spinrobin followed, panting, thinking vaguely of the other employers he had known—philanthropists, bankers, ambitious members of Parliament, and all the rest—commonplace individuals to a man; and then of the immense and towering figure striding just ahead, shedding about him this vibrating atmosphere of power and whirlwind, touched so oddly here and there with a vein of gentleness that was almost sweetness. Never before had he known any human being who radiated such vigour, such big and beneficent fatherliness, yet for all the air of kindliness something, too, that touched in him the sense of awe. Mr. Skale, he felt, was a very unusual man.

They went on in the gathering dusk, talking little but easily. Spinrobin felt "taken care of." Usually he was shy with a new employer, but this man inspired much too large a sensation in him to include shyness, or any other form of petty self-consciousness. He felt more like a son than a secretary. He remembered the wording of the advertisement, the phrases of the singular correspondence—and wondered. "A remarkable personality," he thought to himself as he stumbled through the dark after the object of his reflections; "simple—yet tremendous! A giant in all sorts of ways probably—" Then his thought hesitated, floundered. There was something else he divined yet could not name. He felt out of his depth in some entirely new way, in touch with an order of possibilities larger, more vast, more remote than any dreams his imagination even had yet envisaged. All this, and more, the mere presence of this retired clergyman poured into his receptive and eager little soul.

And very soon it was that these nameless qualities began to assert themselves, completing the rout of Spinrobin's moderate powers of judgement. No practical word as to the work before them, or the duties of the new secretary, had yet passed between them. They walked along together, chatting as equals, acquaintances, almost two friends might have done. And on the top of the hill, after a four-mile trudge, they rested for the first time, Spinrobin panting and perspiring, trousers tucked up and splashed yellow with mud; Mr. Skale, legs apart, beard flattened by the wind about his throat, and thumbs in the slits of his waistcoat as he looked keenly about him over the darkening landscape. Treeless and desolate hills rose on all sides. A few tumbled-down cottages of grey stone lay scattered upon the lower slopes among patches of shabby and forlorn cultivation. Here and there an outcrop of rock ran skywards into sombre and precipitous ridges. The October wind passed to and fro over it all, mournfully singing, and driving loose clouds that seemed to drop weighted shadows among the peaks.

III

And it was here that Mr. Skale stopped abruptly, looked about him, and then down at his companion.

"Bleak and lonely—this great spread of bare mountain and falling cliff," he observed half to himself, half to the other; "but fine, very, very fine." He exhaled deeply, then inhaled as though the great draught of air was profoundly satisfying. He turned to catch his companion's eye. "There's a savage and desolate beauty here that uplifts. It helps the mind to dwell upon the full sweep of life instead of getting dwarfed and lost among its petty details. Pretty scenery is not good for the soul." And again he inhaled a prodigious breastful of the mountain air. "This is."

"But an element of terror in it, perhaps, sir," suggested the secretary who, truth to tell, preferred his scenery more smiling, and who, further, had been made suddenly aware that in this sombre setting of bleak and elemental nature the great figure of his future employer assumed a certain air of grandeur that was a little too awe-inspiring to be pleasant.

"In all profound beauty there must be that," the clergyman was saying; "fine terror, I mean, of course—just enough to bring out the littleness of man by comparison."

"Perhaps, yes," agreed Spinrobin. His own insignificance seemed peculiarly apparent at that moment in contrast to Mr. Skale who had become part and parcel of the rugged landscape. Spinrobin was a lost atom whirling somewhere outside on his own account, whereas the other seemed oddly in touch with it, almost merged and incorporated into it. With those deep breaths the clergyman absorbed something of this latent power about them—then gave it out again. It broke over his companion like a wave. Elemental force of some kind emanated from that massive human figure beside him.

The wind came tearing up the valley and swept past them with a rush as of mighty wings. Mr. Skale drew attention to it. "And listen to that!" he said. "How it leaps, singing, from the woods in the valley up to those gaunt old cliffs yonder!" He pointed. His beard blew suddenly across his face. With his bare head and shaggy flying hair, his big eyes and bold aquiline nose, he presented an impressive figure. Spinrobin watched him with growing amazement, aware that an enthusiasm scarcely warranted by the wind and scenery had passed into his manner. In his own person, too, he thought he experienced a birth of something similar—a little wild rush of delight he was unable to account for. The voice of his companion, pointing out the house in the valley below, again interrupted his thoughts.

"How the mountains positively eat it up. It lies in their very jaws," and the secretary's eyes, travelling into the depths, made out a cluster of grey stone chimneys and a clearing in the woods that evidently represented lawns. The phrase "courage and imagination" flashed unbidden into his mind as he realized the loneliness of the situation, and for the hundredth time he wondered what in the world could be the experiments with sound that this extraordinary man pursued in this isolated old mansion among the hills.

"Buried, sir, rather," he suggested. "I can only just see it—"

"And inaccessible," Mr. Skale interrupted him. "Hard to get at. No one comes to disturb; an ideal place for work. In the hollows of these hills a man may indeed seek truth and pursue it, for the world does not enter here." He paused a moment. "I hope, Mr. Spinrobin," he added, turning towards him with that gentle smile his shaggy visage sometimes wore, "I hope you will not find it too lonely. We have no visitors, I mean; nothing but our own little household of four."

Spinrobin smiled back. Even at this stage he admits he was exceedingly anxious to suit. Mr. Skale, in spite of his marked peculiarities, inspired him with confidence. His personal attraction was growing every minute; that vague awe he roused probably only increased it. He wondered who the "four" might be.

"There's nothing like solitude for serious work, sir," replied the younger man, stifling a passing uneasiness.

And with that they plunged down the hillside into the valley, Mr. Skale leading the way at a terrific pace, shouting out instructions and warnings from time to time that echoed from the rocks as though voices followed them down from the mountains. The darkness swallowed them, they left the wind behind; the silence that dwells in the folded hills fell about their steps; the air grew less keen; the trees multiplied, gathering them in with fingers of mist and shadow. Only the clatter of their boots on the rocky path, and the heavy bass of the clergyman's voice shouting instructions from time to time, broke the stillness. Spinrobin followed the big dark outline in front of him as best he could, stumbling frequently. With countless little hopping steps he dodged along from point to point, a certain lucky nimbleness in his twinkling feet saving him from many a tumble.

"All right behind there?" Mr. Skale would thunder.

"All right, thanks, Mr. Skale," he would reply in his thin tenor, "I'm coming."

"Come along, then!" And on they would go faster than before, till in due course they emerged from the encircling woods and reached the more open ground about the house. Somehow, in the jostling relations of the walk, a freedom of intercourse had been established that no amount of formal talk between four walls could have accomplished. They scraped their dirty boots vigorously on the iron mat.

"Tired?" asked the clergyman, kindly.

"Winded, Mr. Skale, thank you—nothing more," was the reply. He looked up at the square mass of the house looming dark against the sky, and the noise his companion made opening the door—the actual rattle of the iron knob did it—suddenly brought to him a clear realization of two things: First, he understood that the whole way from the station Mr. Skale had been watching him closely, weighing, testing, proving him, though by ways and methods so subtle that they had escaped his observation at the time; secondly, that he was already so caught in the network of this personality, vaster and more powerful than his own, that escape if he desired it would be exceedingly difficult. Like a man in a boat upon the upper Niagara river, he already felt the tug and suction of the current below—the lust of a great adventure drawing him forward. Mr. Skale's hand upon his shoulder as they entered the house was the symbol of *that*. The noise of the door closing behind him was the passing of the last bit of quiet water across which a landing to the bank might still have been possible.

Faint streamers from the dark, inscrutable house of fear reached him even then and left their vague, undecipherable signatures upon the surface of his soul. The forces that vibrated so strangely in the atmosphere of Mr. Skale were already playing about his own person, gathering him in like a garment. Yet while he shuddered, he liked it. Was he not already losing something of his own insignificant and diminutive self?

IV

The clergyman, meanwhile, had closed the heavy door, shutting out the darkness, and now led the way across a large, flagged hall into a room, ablaze with lamp and fire, the walls lined thickly with books, furnished cosily if plainly. The laden tea table, and a kettle hissing merrily on the hob, were pleasant to look upon, but what instantly arrested the gaze of the secretary was the face of the old woman in cap and apron—evidently the housekeeper already referred to as

"Mrs." Mawle—who stood waiting to pour out tea. For about her worn and wrinkled countenance there lay an indefinable touch of something that hitherto he had seen only in pictures of the saints by the old masters. What attracted his attention, and held it so arrestingly, was this singular expression of happiness, aye, of more than mere happiness—of joy and peace and blessed surety, rarely, if ever, seen upon a human face alive, and only here and there suggested behind that mask of repose which death leaves so tenderly upon the features of those few who have lived their lives to noblest advantage.

Spinrobin caught his breath a little, and stared. Aged and lined as it unquestionably was, he caught that ineffable suggestion of radiance about it which proclaimed an inner life that had found itself and was in perfect harmony with outer things: a life based upon certain knowledge and certain hope. It wore a gentle whiteness he could find only one word to describe—glory. And the moment he saw it there flashed across him the recognition that this was what Mr. Skale also possessed. That giant, athletic, vigorous man, and this bent, worn old woman both had it. He wondered with a rush of sudden joy what produced it;—whether it might perhaps one day be his too. The flame of his own spirit leapt within him.

And, so wondering, he turned to look at the clergyman. In the softer light of fire and lamp his face had the appearance of forty rather than sixty as he had first judged; the eyes, always luminous, shone with health and enthusiasm; a great air of youth and vitality glowed about him. It was a fine head with that dominating nose and the shaggy tangle of hair and beard; very big, fatherly and protective he looked, a quite inexpressible air of tenderness mingled in everywhere with the strength. Spinrobin felt immensely drawn to him as he looked. With such a leader he could go anywhere, do anything. There, surely, was a man whose heart was set not upon the things of this world.

An introduction to the housekeeper interrupted his reflections; it did not strike him as at all out of the way; doubtless she was more mother than domestic to the household. At the name of "Mrs." Mawle (courtesy-title, obviously), he rose and bowed, and the old woman, looking from one to the other, smiled becomingly, curtseyed, put her cap straight, and turned to the teapot again. She said nothing.

"The only servant I have, practically," explained the clergyman, "cook, butler, housekeeper and tyrant all in one; and, with her niece, the only other persons in the house besides ourselves. A very simple *ménage*, you see, Mr. Spinrobin. I ought to warn you, too, by-the-by," he added, "that she is almost stone deaf, and has only got the use of one arm, as perhaps you noticed. Her left arm is"—he hesitated for a fraction of a second—"withered."

A passing wonder as to what the niece would be like accompanied the swallowing of his buttered toast and tea, but the personalities of Mr. Skale and his housekeeper had already produced emotions that prevented this curiosity acquiring much strength. He could deal with nothing more just yet. Bewilderment obstructed the way, and in his room before dinner he tried in vain to sort out the impressions that so thickly flooded him, though without any conspicuous degree of success. The walls of his bedroom, like those of corridor and hall, were bare; the furniture solid and old-fashioned; scanty, perhaps, yet more than he was accustomed to; and the spaciousness was very pleasant after the cramped quarters of stuffy London lodgings. He unpacked his few things, arranged them with neat precision in the drawers of the tallboy, counted his shirts, socks, and ties, to see that all was right, and then drew up an armchair and toasted his toes before the comforting fire. He tried to think of many things, and to decide numerous little questions roused by the events of the last few hours; but the only thing, it seems, that really occupied his mind, was the rather overpowering fact that he was—with Mr. Skale and in Mr. Skale's house; that he was there on a month's trial; that the nature of the work in which he was to assist was unknown, immense, singular; and that he was already being weighed in the balances by his uncommon and gigantic employer. In his mind he used this very adjective. There was something about the big clergyman—titanic.

He was in the middle of a somewhat jumbled consideration about "Knowledge of Hebrew—tenor voice—courage and imagination— unworldly," and so forth, when a knock at the door announced Mrs. Mawle who came to inform him that dinner was ready. She stood there, a motherly and pleasant figure in black, and she addressed him in the third person. "If Mr. Spinrobin will please to come down," she said, "Mr. Skale is waiting. Mr. Skale is always *quite* punctual." She always spoke thus, in the third person; she never used the personal pronoun if it could be avoided. She preferred the name direct, it seemed. And as Spinrobin passed her on the way out, she observed further, looking straight into his eyes as she said it: "and should Mr. Spinrobin have need of anything, *that*," indicating it, "is the bell that rings in the housekeeper's room. Mrs. Mawle can see it wag, though she can't hear it. Day or night," she added with a faint curtsey, "and no trouble at all, just as with the other gentlemen—"

So there had been other gentlemen, other secretaries! He thanked her with a nod and a smile, and hurried pattering downstairs in a neat blue suit, black silk socks and a pair of bright new pumps, Mr. Skale having told him not to dress. The phrase "day or night," meanwhile, struck him as significant and peculiar. He remembered it later. At the moment he merely noted that it added one more to the puzzling items that caused his bewilderment.

V

Before he had gone very far, however, there came another—crowningly perplexing. For he was halfway down the darkened passage, making for the hall that glimmered beyond like the mouth of a cave, when, without the smallest warning, he became suddenly conscious that something attractive and utterly delicious had invaded the stream of his being. It came from nowhere—inexplicably, and at first it took the form of a naked sensation of delight, keen as a thrill of boyhood days. There passed into him very swiftly something that satisfied. "I mean, whatever it was," he says, "I couldn't have asked or wanted more of it. It was all there, complete, supreme, sufficient." And the same instant he saw close beside him, in the comparative gloom of the narrow corridor, a vivid, vibrating picture of a girl's face, pale as marble, of flower-like beauty, with dark voluminous hair and large grey eyes that met his own from behind a wavering net of eyelashes. Down to the shoulders he saw her.

Erect and motionless she stood against the wall to let him pass—this slim young girl whose sudden and unexpected presence had so electrified him. Her eyes followed him like those of a picture, but she neither bowed nor curtseyed, and the only movement she made was the slight turning of the head and eyes as he went by. It was extraordinarily effective, this silent and delightful introduction, for swift as lightning, and with lightning's terrific and incalculable surety of aim, she leapt into his heart with the effect of a blinding and complete possession.

It was, of course, he realized, the niece—the fourth member of the household, and the first clear thought to disentangle itself from the resultant jumble of emotions was his instinctive wonder what her name might be. How was this delightful apparition called? This was the question that ran and danced in his blood. In another minute he felt sure he would discover it. It must begin (he felt sure of that) with an M.

He did not pause, or alter his pace. He made no sign of recognition. Their eyes swallowed each other for a brief moment as he passed—and then he was pattering with quick, excited steps down the passage beyond, and the girl was left out of sight in the shadows behind him. He did not even turn back to look, for in some amazing sense she seemed to move on beside him, as though some portion of her had merged into his being. He carried her on with him. Some sweet and marvellous interchange they had undergone together. He felt strangely blessed, soothed inwardly, made complete, and more than twice on the way down the name he knew must belong to her almost sprang up and revealed itself—yet never quite. He knew it began with M, even with Mir—but could get nothing more. The rest evaded him. He divined only a portion of the name. He had seen only a portion of her form.

The first syllable, however, sang in him with an exquisitely sweet authority. He was aware of some glorious new thing in the penetralia of his little spirit, vibrating with happiness. Some portion of himself sang with it. "For it really did vibrate," he said, "and no other word describes it. It vibrated like music, like a string; as though when I passed her she had taken a bow and drawn it across the strings of my inmost being to make them sing..."

"Come," broke in the sonorous voice of the clergyman whom he found standing in the hall; "I've been waiting for you."

It was said, not complainingly nor with any idea of fault-finding, but rather—both tone and manner betrayed it—as a prelude to something of importance about to follow. Somewhat impatiently Mr. Skale took his companion by the arm and led him forwards; on the stone floor Spinrobin's footsteps sounded light and dancing, like a child's. The clergyman strode. At the dining room door he stopped, turning abruptly, and at the same instant the figure of the young girl glided noiselessly towards them from the mouth of the dark corridor where she had been waiting.

Her entry, again, was curiously effective; like a beautiful thought in a dream she moved into the hall, and into Spinrobin's life. Moreover, as she came wholly into view in the light, he felt, as positively as though he heard it uttered, that he knew her name complete. The first syllable had come to him in the passageway when he saw her partly, and the feeling of dread that "Mir—" might prove to be part of "Miranda," "Myrtle," or some other enormity, passed instantly. These would only have been gross and cruel misnomers. Her right name—the only one that described her soul—must end, as it began, with M. It flashed into his mind, and at the same moment Mr. Skale picked it off his very lips.

"Miriam," he said in deep tones, rolling the name along his mouth so as to extract every shade of sound belonging to it, "this is Mr. Spinrobin about whom I told you. He is coming, I hope, to help us."

VI

At first Spinrobin was only aware of the keen delight produced in him by the manner of Skale's uttering her name, for it entered his consciousness with a murmuring, singing sound that continued on in his thoughts like a melody. His racing blood carried it to every portion of his body. He heard her name, not with his ears alone but with his whole person—a melodious, haunting phrase of music that thrilled him exquisitely. Next, he knew that she stood close before him, shaking his hand, and looking straight into his eyes with an expression of the most complete trust and sympathy imaginable, and that he felt a well-nigh irresistible desire to draw her yet closer to him and kiss her little shining face. Thirdly—though the three impressions were as a matter of fact almost simultaneous—that the huge figure of the clergyman stood behind them, watching with the utmost intentness and interest, like a keen and alert detective eager for some betrayal of evidence, inspired, however, not by mistrust, but by a very zealous sympathy.

He understood that this meeting was of paramount importance in Mr. Skale's purpose.

"How do you do, Mr. Spinrobin," he heard a soft voice saying, and the commonplace phrase served to bring him back to a more normal standard of things. But the tone in which she said it caused him a second thrill almost more delightful than the first, for the quality was low and fluty, like the gentle note of some mellow wind instrument, and the caressing way she pronounced his name was a revelation. Mr. Skale had known how to make it sound dignified, but this girl did more—she made it sound alive. "I will give thee a new name" flashed into his thoughts, as some memory-cell of boyhood discharged its little burden most opportunely and proceeded to refill itself.

The smile of happiness that broke over Spinrobin's face was certainly reflected in the eyes that gazed so searchingly into his own, without the smallest sign of immodesty, yet without the least inclination to drop the eyelids. The two natures ran out to meet each other as naturally as two notes of music run to take their places in a chord. This slight, blue-eyed youth, light of hair and sensitive of spirit, and this slim, dark-skinned little maiden, with the voice of music and the wide-open grey eyes, understood one another from the very first instant their atmospheres touched and mingled; and the big Skale, looking on intently over their very shoulders, saw that it was good and smiled down upon them, too, in his turn.

"The harmony of souls and voices is complete," he said, but in so low a tone that the secretary did not hear it. Then, with a hand on a shoulder of each, he half pushed them before him into the dining room, his whole face running, as it were, into a single big smile of contentment. The important event had turned out to his entire satisfaction. He looked like some beneficent father, well pleased with his two children.

But Spinrobin, as he moved beside the girl and heard the rustle of her dress that almost touched him, felt as though he stood upon a sliding platform that was moving ever quicker, and that the adventure upon which he was embarked had now acquired a momentum that nothing he could do would ever stop. And he liked it. It would carry him out of himself into something very big...

And at dinner, where he sat opposite to the girl and studied her face closely, Mr. Skale, he was soon aware, was occupied in studying the two of them even more closely. He appeared always to be listening to their voices. They spoke little enough, however, only their eyes met continually, and when they did so there was no evidence of a desire to withdraw. Their gaze remained fastened on one another, on her part without shyness, without impudence on his. That Mr. Skale wished for them an intimate and even affectionate understanding was evident, and the secretary warmed to him on that account more than ever, if on no other.

It surprised him too—when he thought of it, which was rarely—that a girl who was perforce of humble origin could carry herself with an air of such complete and natural distinction, and prove herself so absolutely "the lady." For there was something about her of greater value than any mere earthly rank or class could confer; her spirit was in its very essence distinguished, perfectly simple, yet strong with a great and natural pride. It never occurred to her soul to doubt its own great value—or to question that of others. She somehow or other made the little secretary feel of great account. He had never quite realized his own value before. Her presence, her eyes, her voice served to bring it out. And a very curious detail that he always mentions just at this point is the fact that it never occurred to him to wonder what her surname might be, or whether, indeed, she had one at all. Her name, Miriam, seemed sufficient. The rest of her—if there was any other part of her not described by those three syllables—lay safely and naturally included somewhere in *his own* name. "Spinrobin" described her as well as himself. But "Miriam" completed his own personality and at the same time extended it. He felt all wrapped up and at peace with her. With Philip Skale, Mrs. Mawle and Miriam, he, Robert Spinrobin, felt that he naturally belonged as "one of the family." They were like the four notes in the chord: Skale, the great bass; Mawle, the mellow alto; himself and Miriam, respectively, the echoing tenor and the singing soprano. The imagery by which, in the depths of his mind, he sought to interpret to himself the whole singular business ran, it seems, even then to music and the analogies of music.

The meal was short and very simple. Mrs. Mawle carved the joint at the end of the table, handed the vegetables and looked after their wants with the precision of long habit. Her skill, in spite of the withered arm, was noteworthy. They talked little, Mr. Skale hardly at all. Miriam spoke from time to time across the table to the secretary. She did not ask questions, she stated facts, as though she already knew all about his feelings and tastes. She may have been twenty years of age, perhaps, but in some way she took him back to childhood. And she said things with the simple audacity of a child, ignoring Mr. Skale's presence. It seemed to the secretary as if he had always known her.

"I knew just how you would look," she said, without a trace of shyness, "the moment I heard your name. And you got my name very quickly, too?"

"Only part of it, at first—"

"Oh yes; but when you saw me completely you got it all," she interrupted. "And I like your name," she added, looking him full in the eye with her soft grey orbs; "it tells everything."

"So does yours, you know."

"Oh, of course," she laughed; "Mr. Skale gave it to me the day I was born."

"I *heard* it," put in the clergyman, speaking almost for the first time. And the talk dropped again, the secretary's head fairly whirling.

"You used it all, of course, as a little boy," she said presently again; "names, I mean?"

"Rather," he replied without hesitation; "only I've rather lost it since—"

"It will come back to you here. It's so splendid, all this world of sound, and makes everything seem worth while. But you lose your way at first, of course; especially if you are out of practice, as you must be."

Spinrobin did not know what to say. To hear this young girl make use of such language took his breath away. He became aware that she was talking with a purpose, seconding Mr. Skale in the secret examination to which the clergyman was all the time subjecting him. Yet there was no element of alarm in it all. In the room with these two, and with the motherly figure of the housekeeper busying about to and fro, he felt at home, comforted, looked after—more even, he felt at his best; as though the stream of his little life were mingling in with a much bigger and worthier river, a river, moreover, in flood. But it was the imagery of music again that most readily occurred to him. He felt that the note of his own little personality had been caught up into the comforting bosom of a complete chord...

VII

"Mr. Spinrobin," suddenly sounded soft and low across the table, and, thrilled to hear the girl speak his name, he looked up quickly and found her very wide-opened eyes peering into his. Her face was thrust forward a little as she leaned over the table in his direction.

As he gazed she repeated his name, leisurely, quietly, and even more softly than before: "Mr. Spinrobin." But this time, as their eyes met and the syllables issued from her lips, he noticed that a singular after-sound—an exceedingly soft yet vibrant overtone—accompanied it. The syllables set something quivering within him, something that sang, running of its own accord into a melody to which his rising pulses beat time and tune.

"Now, please, speak my name," she added. "Please look straight at me, straight into my eyes, and pronounce *my* name."

His lips trembled, if ever so slightly, as he obeyed.

"Miriam..." he said.

"Pronounce each syllable very distinctly and very slowly," she said, her grey eyes all over his burning face.

"Mir... i... am," he repeated, looking in the centre of the eyes without flinching, and becoming instantly aware that his utterance of the name produced in himself a development and extension of the original overtones awakened by her speaking of his own name. It was wonderful... exquisite... delicious. He uttered it again, and then heard that she, too, was uttering his at the same moment. Each spoke the other's name. He could have sworn he heard the music within him leap across the intervening space and transfer itself to her... and that he heard his own name singing, too, in *her* blood.

For the names were true. By this soft intoning utterance they seemed to pass mutually into the secret rhythm of that Eternal Principle of Speech which exists behind the spoken sound and is independent of its means of manifestation. Their central beings, screened and limited behind their names, knew an instant of synchronous rhythmical vibration. It was their introduction absolute to one another, for it was an instant of naked revelation.

"Spinrobin..."

"Miriam..."

VIII

... A great volume of sound suddenly enveloped and caught away the two singing names, and the spell was broken. Miriam dropped her eyes; Spinrobin looked up. It was Mr. Skale's voice upon them with a shout.

"Splendid! splendid!" he cried; "your voices, like your names, are made for one another, in quality, pitch, accent, everything." He was enthusiastic rather than excited; but to Spinrobin, taking part in this astonishing performance, to which the other two alone held the key, it all seemed too perplexing for words. The great bass crashed and boomed for a moment about his ears; then came silence. The test, or whatever it was, was over. It had been successful.

Mr. Skale, his face still shining with enthusiasm, turned towards him. Miriam, equally happy, watched, her hands folded in her lap.

"My dear fellow," exclaimed the clergyman, half rising in his chair, "how mad you must think us! How mad you must think us! I can only assure you that when you know more, as you soon shall, you will understand the importance of what has just taken place..."

He said a good deal more that Spinrobin did not apparently quite take in. He was too bewildered. His eyes sought the girl where she sat opposite, gazing at him. For all its pallor, her face was tenderly soft and beautiful; more pure and undefiled, he thought, than any human countenance he had ever seen, and sweet as the face of a child. Utterly unstained it was. A similar light shone in the faces of Skale and Mrs. Mawle. In their case it had forged its way through the more or less defiling garment of a worn and experienced flesh. But the light in Miriam's eyes and skin was there because it had never been extinguished. She had retained her pristine brilliance of soul. Through the little spirit of the perplexed secretary ran a thrill of genuine worship and adoration.

"Mr. Skale's coffee is served in the library," announced the voice of the housekeeper abruptly behind them; and when Spinrobin turned again he discovered that Miriam had slipped from the room unobserved and was gone.

Mr. Skale took his companion's arm and led the way towards the hall.

"I am glad you love her," was his astonishing remark. "It is the first and most essential condition of your suiting me."

"She is delightful, wonderful, charming, sir—"

"Not 'sir,' if you please," replied the clergyman, standing aside at the threshold for his guest to pass; "I prefer the use of the name, you know. I think it is important."

And he closed the library door behind them.

I

For some minutes they sat in front of the fire and sipped their coffee in silence. The secretary felt that the sliding platform on which he was travelling into this extraordinary adventure had been going a little too fast for him. Events had crowded past before he had time to look squarely at them. He had lost his bearings rather, routed by Miriam's beauty and by the amazing way she talked to him. Had she lived always inside his thoughts she could not have chosen words better calculated to convince him that they were utterly in sympathy one with the other. Mr. Skale, moreover, approved heartily. The one thing Spinrobin saw clearly through it all was that himself and Miriam—their voices, rather—were necessary for the success of the clergyman's mysterious experiments. Only, while Miriam, little witch, knew all about it, he, candidate on trial, knew as yet—nothing.

And now, as they sat opposite one another in the privacy of the library, Spinrobin, full of confidence and for once proud of his name and personality, looked forward to being taken more into the heart of the affair. Things advanced, however, more slowly than he desired. Mr. Skale's scheme was too big to be hurried.

The clergyman did not smoke, but his companion, with the other's ready permission, puffed gently at a small cigarette. Short, rapid puffs he took, as though the smoke was afraid to enter beyond the front teeth, and with one finger he incessantly knocked off the ashes into his saucer, even when none were there to fall. On the table behind them gurgled the shaded lamp, lighting their faces from the eyes downwards.

"Now," said Mr. Skale, evidently not aware that he thundered, "we can talk quietly and undisturbed." He caught his beard in a capacious hand, in such a way that the square outline of his chin showed through the hair. His voice boomed musically, filling the room. Spinrobin listened acutely, afraid even to cross his legs. A genuine pronouncement, he felt, was coming.

"A good many years ago, Mr. Spinrobin," he said simply, "when I was a curate of a country parish in Norfolk, I made a discovery—of a revolutionary description—a discovery in the world of real things, that is, of spiritual things."

He gazed fixedly over the clutched beard at his companion, apparently searching for brief, intelligible phrases. "But a discovery, the development of which I was obliged to put on one side until I inherited with this property the means and leisure which enabled me to continue my terrific—I say purposely terrific—researches. For some years now I have been quietly at work here absorbed in my immense pursuit." And again he stopped. "I have reached a point, Mr. Spinrobin—"

"Yes," interjected the secretary, as though the mention of his name touched a button and produced a sound. "A point—?"

"Where I need the assistance of some one with a definite quality of voice—a man who emits a certain note—a certain tenor note." He released his beard, so that it flew out with a spring, at the same moment thrusting his head forward to drive home the announcement effectively.

Spinrobin crossed his legs with a fluttering motion, hastily. "As you advertised," he suggested.

The clergyman bowed.

"My efforts to find the right man," continued the enthusiast, leaning back in his chair, "have now lasted a year. I have had a dozen men down here, each on a month's trial. None of them suited. None had the requisite quality of voice. With a single exception, none of them could stand the loneliness, the seclusion; and without exception, all of them were too worldly to make sacrifices. It was the salary they wanted. The majority, moreover, confused imagination with fancy, and courage with mere audacity. And, most serious of all, not one of them passed the test of—Miriam. She harmonized with none of them. They were discords one and all. You, Mr. Spinrobin, are the first to win acceptance. The instant she heard your name she cried for you. And she knows. She sings the soprano. She took you into the chord."

"I hope indeed—" stammered the flustered and puzzled secretary, and then stopped, blushing absurdly. "You claim for me far more than I should dare to claim for myself," he added. The reference to Miriam delighted him, and utterly destroyed his judgement. He longed to thank the girl for having approved him. "I'm glad my voice—er—suits your—chord." In his heart of hearts he understood something of what Mr. Skale was driving at, yet was half-ashamed to admit it even to himself. In this twentieth century it all seemed so romantic, mystical, and absurd. He felt it was all half-true. If only he could have run back into that great "mental prairie" of his boyhood days it might all have been *quite* true.

"Precisely," continued Mr. Skale, bringing him back to reality, "precisely. And now, before I tell you more, you will forgive my asking you one or two personal questions, I'm sure. We must build securely as we go, leaving nothing to chance. The grandeur and importance of my experiments demand it. Afterwards," and his expression changed to a sudden softness in a way that was characteristic of the man, "you must feel free to put similar questions to me, as personal and direct as you please. I wish to establish a perfect frankness between us at the start."

"Thank you, Mr. Skale. Of course—er—should anything occur to me to ask—" A momentary bewilderment, caused by the great visage so close to his own, prevented the completion of the sentence.

"As to your beliefs, for instance," the clergyman resumed abruptly, "your religious beliefs, I mean. I must be sure of you on that ground. What are you?"

"Nothing—I think," Spinrobin replied without hesitation, remembering how his soul had bounced its way among the various creeds since Cambridge, and arrived at its present state of Belief in Everything, yet without any definite label. "Nothing in particular. Nominally, though—a Christian."

"You believe in a God?"

"A Supreme Intelligence, most certainly," was the emphatic reply.

"And spirits?"

Spinrobin hesitated. He was a very honest soul.

"Other life, let me put it," the clergyman helped him; "other beings besides ourselves?"

"I have often felt—wondered, rather," he answered carefully, "whether there might not be other systems of evolution besides humanity. Such extraordinary Forces come blundering into one's life sometimes, and one can't help wondering where they come from. I have never formulated any definite beliefs, however—"

"Your world is not a blind chaos, I mean?" Mr. Skale put gravely to him, as though questioning a child.

"No, no, indeed. There's order and system—"

"In which you personally count for something of value?" asked the other quickly.

"I like to think so," was the apologetic reply. "There's something that includes me somewhere in a purpose of very great importance—only, of course, I've got to do my part, and—"

"Good," Mr. Skale interrupted him. "And now," he asked softly, after a moment's pause, leaning forward, "what about death? Are you afraid of death?"

Spinrobin started visibly. He began to wonder where this extraordinary catechism was going to lead. But he answered at once: he had thought out these things and knew where he stood.

"Only of its possible pain," he said, smiling into the bearded visage before him. "And an immense curiosity, of course—"

"It does not mean extinction for you—going out like the flame of a candle, for instance?"

"I have never been able to believe *that*, Mr. Skale. I continue somewhere and somehow—forever."

The cross-examination puzzled him more and more, and through it, for the first time, he began to feel dimly, ran a certain strain of something not quite right, not permissible in the biggest sense. It was not the questions themselves that produced this odd and rather disquieting impression, but the fact that Mr. Skale was preparing the ground with such extraordinary thoroughness. This conversation was the first swell, as it were, rolling mysteriously in upon him from the ocean in whose deeps the great Experiment lay buried. Forces, tidal in strength, oceanic in volume, shrouded it just now, but he already felt them. They reached him through the person of the clergyman. It was these forces playing through his personality that Spinrobin had been aware of the first moment they met on the station platform, and had "sensed" even more strongly during the walk home across the mountains.

Behind the play of these darker impressions, as yet only vague and ambiguous, there ran in and out among his thoughts the vein of something much sweeter. Miriam, with her large grey eyes and silvery voice, was continually peeping in upon his mind. He wondered where she was and what she was doing in the big, lonely house. He wished she could have been in the room to hear his answers and approve them. He felt incomplete without her. Already he thought of her as the melody to which he was the accompaniment, two things that ought not to be separated.

"My point is," Mr. Skale continued, "that, apart from ordinary human ties, and so forth, you have no intrinsic terror of death—of losing your present body?"

"No, no," was the reply, more faintly given than the rest. "I love my life, but—but—" he looked about him in some confusion for the right words, still thinking of Miriam—"but I look forward, Mr. Skale; I look forward." He dropped back into the depths of his armchair and puffed swiftly at the end of his extinguished cigarette, oblivious of the fact that no smoke came.

"The attitude of a brave man," said the clergyman with approval. Then, looking straight into the secretary's blue eyes, he added with increased gravity: "And therefore it would not be immoral of me to expose you to an experiment in which the penalty of a slip would be—death? Or you would not shrink from it yourself, provided the knowledge to be obtained seemed worth while?"

"That's right, sir—Mr. Skale, I mean; that's right," came the answer after an imperceptible pause.

The result of the talk seemed to satisfy the clergyman. "You must think my questions *very* peculiar," he said, the sternness of his face relaxing a little, "but it was necessary to understand your exact position before proceeding further. The gravity of my undertaking demands it. However, you must not let my words alarm you." He waited a moment, reflecting deeply. "You must regard them, if you will, as a kind of test," he resumed, searching his companion's face with eagle eyes, "the beginning of a series of tests in which your attitude to Miriam and hers to you, so far as that goes, was the first."

"Oh, that's all right, Mr. Skale," was his inadequate rejoinder; for the moment the name of the girl was introduced his thoughts instantly wandered out to find her. The way the clergyman pronounced it increased its power, too, for no name he uttered sounded ordinary. There seemed a curious mingling in the resonant cavity of his great mouth of the fundamental note and the overtones.

"Yes, you have the kind of courage that is necessary," Mr. Skale was saying, half to himself, "the modesty that forgets self, and the unworldly attitude that is essential. With your help I may encompass success; and I consider myself wonderfully fortunate to have found you, wonderfully fortunate..."

"I'm glad," murmured Spinrobin, thinking that so far he had not learned anything very definite about his duties, or what it was he had to do to earn so substantial a salary. Truth to tell, he did not bother much about that part of it. He was conscious only of three main desires: to pass the unknown tests, to learn the nature of Mr. Skale's discovery, with the experiment involved, and—to be with Miriam as much as possible. The whole affair was so unusual that he had already lost the common standards of judging. He let the sliding platform take him where it would, and he flattered himself that he was not fool enough to mistake originality for insanity. The clergyman, dreamer and enthusiast though he might be, was as sane as other men, saner than most.

"I hope to lead you little by little to what I have in view," Mr. Skale went on, "so that at the end of our trial month you will have learned enough to enable you to form a decision, yet not enough to—to use my knowledge should you choose to return to the world."

It was very frank, but the secretary did not feel offended. He accepted the explanation as perfectly reasonable. In his mind he knew full well what his choice would be. This was the supreme adventure he had been so long a-seeking. No ordinary obstacle could prevent his accepting it.

II

There came a pause of some length, in which Spinrobin found nothing particular to say. The lamp gurgled; the coals fell softly into the fender. Then suddenly Mr. Skale rose and stood with his back to the grate. He gazed down upon the small figure in the chair. He towered there, a kindly giant, enthusiasm burning in his eyes like lamps. His voice was very deep, his manner more solemn than before when he spoke.

"So far, so good," he said, "and now, with your permission, Mr. Spinrobin, I should like to go a step further. I should like to take— your note."

"My note?" exclaimed the other, thinking he had not heard correctly.

"Your sound, yes," repeated the clergyman.

"My sound!" piped the little man, vastly puzzled, his voice shrill with excitement. He dodged about in the depths of his big leather chair, as though movement might bring explanation.

Mr. Skale watched him calmly. "I want to get the vibrations of your voice, and then see what pattern they produce in the sand," he said.

"Oh, in the sand, yes; quite so," replied the secretary. He remembered how the vibrations of an elastic membrane can throw dry sand, loosely scattered upon its surface, into various floral and geometrical figures. Chladni's figures, he seemed to remember, they were called after their discoverer. But Mr. Skale's purpose in the main, of course, escaped him.

"You don't object?"

"On the contrary, I am greatly interested." He stood up on the mat beside his employer.

"I wish to make *quite* sure," the clergyman added gravely, "that your voice, your note, is what I think it is—accurately in harmony with mine and Miriam's and Mrs. Mawle's. The pattern it makes will help to prove this."

The secretary bowed in perplexed silence, while Mr. Skale crossed the room and took a violin from its case. The golden varnish of its ribs and back gleamed in the lamplight, and when the clergyman drew the bow across the strings to tune it, smooth, mellow sounds, soft and resonant as bells, filled the room. Evidently he knew how to handle the instrument. The notes died away in a murmur.

"A Guarnerius," he explained, "and a perfect pedigree specimen; it has the most sensitive structure imaginable, and carries vibrations almost like a human nerve. For instance, while I speak," he added, laying the violin upon his companion's hand, "you will feel the vibrations of my voice run through the wood into your palm."

"I do," said Spinrobin. It trembled like a living thing.

"Now," continued Mr. Skale, after a pause, "what I first want is to receive the vibrations of your own voice in the same way—into my very pulses. Kindly read aloud steadily while I hold it. Stop reading when I make a sign. I'll nod, so that the vibrations of my voice won't interfere." And he handed a notebook to him with quotations entered neatly in his own handwriting, selected evidently with a purpose, and all dealing with sound, music, as organized sound, and names. Spinrobin read aloud; the first quotation from Meredith he recognized, but the others, and the last one, discussing names, were new to him:—

"But *listen in the thought*; so may there come
Conception of a newly-added chord,
Commanding space beyond where ear has home.

"Everything that the sun shines upon sings or can be made to sing, and can be heard to sing. Gases, impalpable powders, and woollen stuffs, in common with other non-conductors of sound, give forth notes of different pitches when played upon by an intermittent beam of white light. Coloured stuffs will sing in lights of different colours, but refuse to sing in others. The polarization of light being now accomplished, light and sound are known to be alike. Flames have a modulated voice and can be made to sing a definite melody. Wood, stone, metal, skins, fibres, membranes, every rapidly vibrating substance, *all have in them the potentialities of musical sound*.

"Radium receives its energy from, and responds to, radiations which traverse all space—as piano strings respond to sounds in unison with their notes. Space is all a-quiver with waves of radiant energy. We vibrate in sympathy with a few strings here and there—with the tiny X-rays, actinic rays, light waves, heat waves, and the huge electromagnetic waves of Hertz and Marconi; but there are great spaces, numberless radiations, to which we are stone deaf. Some day, a thousand years hence, we shall know the full sweep of this magnificent harmony.

"Everything in nature has its name, and he who has the power to call a thing by its proper name can make it subservient to his will; for its proper name is not the arbitrary name given to it by man, but the expression of the totality of its powers and attributes, because the powers and attributes of each Being are intimately connected with its means of expression, and between both exists the most exact proportion in regard to measure, time, and condition."

The meaning of the four quotations, as he read them, plunged down into him and touched inner chords very close to his own beliefs. Something of his own soul, therefore, passed into his voice as he read. He read, that is to say, with authority.

A nod from Mr. Skale stopped him just as he was beginning a fifth passage. Raising the vibrating instrument to his ear, the clergyman first listened a moment intently. Then he quickly had it under his chin, beard flowing over it like water, and the bow singing across the strings. The note he played—he drew it out with that whipping motion of the bow only possible to a loving expert—was soft and beautiful, long drawn out with a sweet singing quality. He took it on the G string with the second finger—in the "fourth position." It thrilled through him, Spinrobin declares, most curiously and delightfully. It made him happy to hear it. It was very similar to the singing vibrations he had experienced when Miriam gazed into his eyes and spoke his name.

"Thank you," said Mr. Skale, and laid the violin down again. "I've got the note. You're E flat."

"E flat!" gasped Spinrobin, not sure whether he was pleased or disappointed.

"That's your sound, yes. You're E flat—just as I thought, just as I hoped. You fit in exactly. It seems too good to be true!" His voice began to boom again, as it always did when he was moved. He was striding about, very alert, very masterful, pushing the furniture out of his way, his eyes more luminous than ever. "It's magnificent." He stopped abruptly and looked at the secretary with a gaze so enveloping that Spinrobin for an instant lost his bearings altogether. "It means, my dear Spinrobin," he said slowly, with a touch of solemnity that woke an involuntary shiver deep in his listener's being, "that you are destined to play a part, and an important part, in one of the grandest experiments ever dreamed of by the heart of man. For the first time since my researches began twenty years ago I now see the end in sight."

"Mr. Skale—that *is* something—indeed," was all the little man could find to say.

There was no reason he could point to why the words should have produced a sense of chill about his heart. It was only that he felt again the huge groundswell of this vast unknown experiment surging against him, lifting him from his feet—as a man might feel the Atlantic swells rise with him towards the stars before they engulfed him forever. It seemed getting a trifle out of hand, this adventure. Yet it was what he had always longed for, and his courage must hold firm. Besides, Miriam was involved in it with him. What could he ask better than to risk his insignificant personality in some gigantic, mad attempt to plumb the Unknown, with that slender, little pale-faced Beauty by his side? The wave of Mr. Skale's enthusiasm swept him away deliciously.

"And now," he cried, "we'll get your Pattern too. I no longer have any doubts, but none the less it will be a satisfaction to us both to see it. It must, I'm sure, harmonize with ours; it must!"

He opened a cupboard drawer and produced a thin sheet of glass, upon which he next poured some finely powdered sand out of a paper bag. It rattled, dry and faint, upon the smooth, hard surface. And while he did this, he talked rapidly, boomingly, with immense enthusiasm.

"All sounds," he said, half to himself, half to the astonished secretary, "create their own patterns. Sound builds; sound destroys; and invisible sound-vibrations affect concrete matter. For all sounds produce forms—the forms that correspond to them, as you shall now see. Within every form lies the silent sound that first called it into view—into visible shape—into being. Forms, shapes, bodies are the vibratory activities of *sound made visible*."

"My goodness!" exclaimed Spinrobin, who was listening like a man in a dream, but who caught the violence of the clergyman's idea none the less.

"Forms and bodies are—*solidified Sound*," cried the clergyman in italics.

"You say something extraordinary," exclaimed the commonplace Spinrobin in his shrill voice. "Marvellous!" Vaguely he seemed to remember that Schelling had called architecture "frozen music."

Mr. Skale turned and looked at him as a god might look at an insect—that he loved.

"Sound, Mr. Spinrobin," he said, with a sudden and effective lowering of his booming voice, "is the original divine impulse behind nature—communicated to language. It is—creative!"

Then, leaving the secretary with this nut of condensed knowledge to crack as best he could, the clergyman went to the end of the room in three strides. He busied himself for a moment with something upon the wall; then he suddenly turned, his great face aglow, his huge form erect, fixing his burning eyes upon his distracted companion.

"In the Beginning," he boomed solemnly, in tones of profound conviction, "was—the *Word*." He paused a moment, and then continued, his voice filling the room to the very ceiling. "At the Word of God—at the thunder of the Voice of God, worlds leaped into being!" Again he paused. "Sound," he went on, the whole force of his great personality in the phrase, "was the primordial, creative energy. A sound can call a form into existence. Forms are the Sound-Figures of archetypal forces—the Word made Flesh." He stopped, and moved with great soft strides about the room.

Spinrobin caught the words full in the face. For a space he could not measure—considerably less than a second, probably—the consciousness of something unutterably immense, unutterably flaming, rushed tumultuously through his mind, with wings that bore his imagination to a place where light was—dazzling, white beyond words. He felt himself tossed up to Heaven on the waves of a great sea, as the body of strange belief behind the clergyman's words poured through him... For somewhere, behind the incoherence of the passionate language, burned the blaze of a true thought at white heat—could he but grasp it through the stammering utterance.

Then, with equal swiftness, it passed. His present surroundings came back. He dropped with a dizzy rush from awful spaces... and was aware that he was merely—standing on the black, woolly mat before the fire watching the movements of his new employer, that his pumps were bright and pointed, his head just level with a dark marble mantelpiece. Dazed, and a trifle breathless he felt; and at the back of his disordered mind stirred a schoolboy's memory that the Pythagoreans believed the universe to have been called out of chaos by Sound, Number, and Harmony—or something to that effect... But these huge, fugitive thoughts that tore through him refused to be seized and dealt with. He staggered a little, mentally; then, with a prodigious effort, controlled himself—and watched.

III

Mr. Skale, he saw, had fastened the little sheet of glass by its four corners to silken strings hanging from the ceiling. The glass plate hung, motionless and horizontal, in the air with its freight of sand. For several minutes the clergyman played a series of beautiful modulations in double-stopping upon the violin. In these the dominating influence was E flat. Spinrobin was not musical enough to describe it more accurately than this. Only, with greater skill than he knows, he mentions how Skale drew out of that fiddle the peculiarly intimate and searching tones by which strings can reach the spiritual centre of a man and make him respond to delicate vibrations of thoughts beyond his normal gamut...

Spinrobin, listening, understood that he was a greater man than he knew...

And the sand on the glass sheet, he next became aware, was shifting, moving, dancing. He heard the tiny hissing and rattling of the dry grains. It was uncommonly weird. This visible and practical result made the clergyman's astonishing words seem true and convincing. That moving sand brought sanity, yet a certain curious terror of the unknown into it all.

A minute later Mr. Skale stopped playing and beckoned to him.

"See," he said quietly, pointing to the arrangement the particles of sand had assumed under the influence of the vibrations. "There's your pattern—your sound made visible. That's your utterance—the Note you substantially represent and body forth in terms of matter."

The secretary stared. It was a charming but very simple pattern the lines of sand had assumed, not unlike the fronds of a delicate fern growing out of several small circles round the base.

"So that's my note—made visible!" he exclaimed under his breath. "It's delightful; it's quite exquisite."

"That's E flat," returned Mr. Skale in a whisper, so as not to disturb the pattern; "if I altered the note, the pattern would alter too. E natural, for instance, would be different. Only, luckily, you are E flat—just the note we want. And now," he continued, straightening himself up to his full height, "come over and see mine and Miriam's and Mrs. Mawle's, and you'll understand what I meant when I said that yours would harmonize." And in a glass case across the room they examined a number of square sheets of glass with sand upon them in various patterns, all rendered permanent by a thin coating of a glue-like transparent substance that held the particles in position.

"There you see mine and Miriam's and Mrs. Mawle's," he said, stooping to look. "They harmonize most beautifully, you observe, with your own."

It was, indeed, a singular and remarkable thing. The patterns, though all different, yet combined in some subtle fashion impossible of analysis to form a complete and well-proportioned Whole—a design—a picture. The patterns of the clergyman and the housekeeper provided the base and foreground, those of Miriam and the secretary the delicate superstructure. The girl's pattern, he noted with a subtle pleasure, was curiously similar to his own, but far more delicate and waving. Yet, whereas his was floral, hers was stellar in character; that of the housekeeper was spiral, and Mr. Skale's he could only describe as a miniature whirlwind of very exquisite design rising out of apparently three separate centres of motion.

"If I could paint over them the colour each shade of sound represents," Mr. Skale resumed, "the tint of each *timbre*, or *Klangfarbe*, as the Germans call it, you would see better still how we are all grouped together there into a complete and harmonious whole."

Spinrobin looked from the patterns to his companion's great face bending there beside him. Then he looked back again at the patterns. He could think of nothing quite intelligible to say. He noticed more clearly every minute that these dainty shapes of sand, stellar, spiral, and floral, stood to one another in certain definite proportions, in a rising and calculated ratio of singular beauty.

"There, before you, lies a true and perfect chord made visible," the clergyman said in tones thrilling with satisfaction, "—three notes in harmony with the fundamental sound, myself, and with each other. My dear fellow, I congratulate you, I congratulate you."

"Thank you very much, indeed," murmured Spinrobin. "I don't quite understand it all yet, but it's—it's extraordinarily fascinating and wonderful."

Mr. Skale said nothing, and Spinrobin drifted back to his big armchair. A deep silence pervaded the room for the space of several minutes. In the heart of that silence lay the mass of direct and vital questions the secretary burned, yet was afraid, to ask. For such was the plain truth; he yearned to know, yet feared to hear. The Discovery and the Experiment of this singular man loomed already somewhat vast and terrible; the adjective that had suggested itself before returned to him—"not permissible."... Of Mr. Skale himself he had no sort of fear, though a growing and uncommon respect, but of the purpose Mr. Skale had in view he caught himself thinking more and more, yet without obvious reason, with a distinct shrinking almost amounting to dismay. But for the fact that so sweet and gentle a creature as Miriam was travelling the same path with him, this increased sense of caution would have revealed itself plainly for what it was—Fear...

"I am deeply interested, Mr. Skale," he said at length, breaking first the silence, "and sympathetic too, I assure you; only—you will forgive me for saying it—I am, as yet, still rather in the dark as to where all this is to lead—" The clergyman's eyes, fixed straight upon his own, again made it difficult to finish the sentence as he wished.

"Necessarily so, because I can only lead you to my discovery step by step," replied the other steadily. "I wish you to be thoroughly prepared for anything that may happen, so that you can deal intelligently with results that might otherwise overwhelm you."

"Overwhelm—?" faltered his listener.

"*Might*, I said. Note carefully my use of words, for they are accurately chosen. Before I can tell you all I must submit you, for your own sake, to certain tests—chiefly to the test of Alteration of Form by Sound. It is somewhat—er—alarming, I believe, the first time. You must be thoroughly accustomed to these astonishing results before we dare to approach the final Experiment; so that you will not tremble. For there can be no rehearsal. The great Experiment can only be made once... and I must be as sure as possible that you will feel no terror in the face of the Unknown."

IV

Spinrobin listened breathlessly. He hesitated a moment after the other stopped speaking, then slewed round on his slippery chair and faced him.

"I can understand," he began, "why you want imagination, but you spoke of courage too? I mean,—is there any immediate cause for alarm? Any personal danger, for instance, *now*?" For the clergyman's weighty sentences had made him realize in a new sense the loneliness of his situation here among these desolate hills. He would appreciate some assurance that his life was not to be trifled with before he lost the power to withdraw if he wished to do so.

"None whatever," replied Mr. Skale with decision, "there is no question at all of physical personal injury. You must trust me and have a little patience." His tone and manner were exceedingly grave, yet at the same time inspired confidence.

"I do," said Spinrobin honestly.

Another pause fell between them, longer than the rest; it was broken by the clergyman. He spoke emphatically, evidently weighing his words with the utmost care.

"This Chord," he said simply—yet, for all the simplicity, there ran to and fro behind his words the sense of unlawful and immense forces impending—"I need for a stupendous experiment with sound, an experiment which will lead in turn towards a yet greater and final one. There is no harm in your knowing that. To produce a certain transcendent result I want a complex sound—a chord, but a complete and perfect chord in which each note is sure of itself and absolutely accurate."

He waited a moment. There was utter silence about them in the room. Spinrobin held his breath.

"No instrument can help me; the notes must be human," he resumed in a lower voice, "and the utterers—pure. For the human voice can produce sounds 'possessing in some degree the characteristics not only of all musical instruments, but of all sounds of whatever description.' By means of this chord I hope to utter a certain sound, a certain *name*, of which you shall know more hereafter. But a name, as you surely know, need not be composed of one or two syllables only; a whole symphony may be a name, and a whole orchestra playing for days, or an entire nation chanting for years, may be required to pronounce the beginning merely of—of certain names. Yours, Robert Spinrobin, for instance, I can pronounce in a quarter of a second; but there may be names so vast, so mighty, that minutes, days, years even, may be necessary for their full utterance. There may be names, indeed, which can never be known, for they could never be uttered—*in time*. For the moment I am content simply to drop this thought into your consciousness; later you shall understand more. I only wish you to take in now that I need this perfect chord for the utterance in due course of a certain complex and stupendous name—the invocation, that is, of a certain complex and stupendous Force!"

"I think I understand," whispered the other, afraid to interrupt more.

"And the difficulty I have experienced in finding the three notes has been immense. I found Mrs. Mawle—alto; then Miriam I found at birth and trained her—soprano; and now I have found you, Mr. Spinrobin, and my chord, with myself as bass, is complete. Your note and Miriam's, soprano and tenor, are closer than the relations between the other notes, and a tenor has accordingly been most difficult to find. You can now understand the importance of your being sympathetic to each other."

Spinrobin's heart burned within him as he listened. He began to grasp some sweet mystical meaning in the sense of perfect companionship the mere presence of the girl inspired. They were the upper notes in the same chord together, linked in a singing and harmonious relation, the one necessary to the other. Moreover, in the presence of Mr. Skale and the housekeeper, bass and alto in the full chord, their completeness was still more emphasized, and they knew their fullest life. The adventure promised to be amazingly seductive. He would learn practically the strange truth that to know the highest life Self must be lost and merged in something bigger. And was this not precisely what he had so long been seeking—escape from his own insignificance?

"And—er—the Hebrew that you require of me, Mr. Skale?" he asked, returning to practical considerations.

"Our purposes require a certain knowledge of Hebrew," he answered without hesitation or demur, "because that ancient language and the magical resources of sound are profoundly linked. In the actual sounds of many of the Hebrew letters lies a singular power, unguessed by the majority, undivined especially, of course, by the mere scholar, but available for the pure in heart who may discover how to use their extraordinary values. They constitute, in my view at least, a remnant of the original Chaldaean mysteries, the lore of that magic which is older than religion. The secret of this knowledge lies in the *psychic values of sound*; for Hebrew, the Hebrew of the Bahir, remains in the hierarchy of languages a direct channel to the unknown and inscrutable forces; and the knowledge of mighty and supersensual things lies locked up in the correct utterance of many of its words, letters and phrases. Its correct utterance, mark well. For knowledge of the most amazing and terrible kind is there, waiting release by him who knows, and who greatly dares.

"And you shall later learn that sound is power. The Hebrew alphabet you must know intimately, and the intricate association of its letters with number, colour, harmony and geometrical form, all of which are but symbols of the Realities at the very roots of life. The Hebrew alphabet, Mr. Spinrobin, is a 'discourse in methods of manifestation, of formation.' In its correct pronunciation lies a way to direct knowledge of divine powers, and to conditions beyond this physical existence."

The clergyman's voice grew lower and lower as he proceeded, and the conviction was unavoidable that he referred to things whereof he had practical knowledge. To Spinrobin it was like the lifting of a great veil. As a boy he had divined something of these values of sound and name, but with the years this knowledge had come to seem fantastic and unreal. It now returned upon him with the force of a terrific certainty. That immense old inner playground of his youth, without boundaries or horizon, rolled up before his mental vision, inviting further and detailed discovery.

"With the language, qua language," he continued, "you need not trouble, but the 'Names' of many things you must know accurately, and especially the names of the so-called 'Angels'; for these are in reality Forces of immense potency, vast spiritual Powers, Qualities, and the like, all evocable by correct utterance of their names. This language, as you will see, is *alive* and divine in the true sense; its letters are the vehicles of activities; its words, terrific formulae; and the true pronunciation of them remains today a direct channel to divine knowledge. In time you shall see; in time you shall know; in time you shall hear. Mr. Spinrobin," and he thrust his great head forwards and dropped his voice to a hushed whisper, "in time we shall all together make this Experiment in sound which shall redeem us and make us as Gods!"

"Thank you!" gasped the secretary, swept off his feet by this torrent of uncommon and mystical language, and passing a moist hand through his feathery hair. He was not entirely ignorant, of course, of the alleged use of sound in the various systems of so-called magic that have influenced the minds of imaginative men during the history of the world. He had heard, more or less vaguely, perhaps, but still with understanding, about "Words of Power"; but hitherto he had merely regarded such things as picturesque superstitions, or half-truths that lie midway between science and imagination. Here, however, was a man in the twentieth century, the days of radium, flying machines, wireless telegraphy, and other invitations towards materialism, who apparently had practical belief in the effective use of sound and in its psychic and divine possibilities, and who was devoting all of his not inconsiderable powers of heart and mind to their actual demonstration. It was astonishing. It was delightful. It was incredible! And, but for the currents of a strange and formidable fear that this conception of Skale's audacious Experiment set stirring in his soul, Spinrobin's enthusiasm would have been possibly as great as his own.

As it was he went up to the big clergyman and held out his hand, utterly carried away by the strangeness of it all, caught up in a vague splendour he did not quite understand, prepared to abandon himself utterly.

"I gather something of what you mean," he said earnestly, "if not all; and I hope most sincerely I may prove suitable for your purpose when the time comes. As a boy, you know, curiously enough, I always believed in the efficacy of names and the importance of naming true. I think," he added somewhat diffidently, looking up straight into the luminous eyes above him, "if you will allow me to say so, I would follow you anywhere, Mr. Skale—anywhere you cared to lead."

"'Upon him that overcometh,'" said the clergyman in that gentle voice he sometimes used, soft as the voice of woman, "'will I write my new name...'"

He gazed down very searchingly into the other's eyes for a minute or two, then shook the proffered hand without another word. And so they separated and went to bed, for it was long past midnight.

I

In his bedroom, though excitement banished sleep in spite of the lateness of the hour, he was too exhausted to make any effective attempt to reduce the confusion of his mind to order. For the first time in his life the diary-page for the day remained blank. For a long time he sat before it with his pencil—then sighed and put it away. A volume he might have written, but not a page, much less a line or two. And though it was but eight hours since he had made the acquaintance of the Rev. Philip Skale, it seemed to him more like eight days.

Moreover, all that he had heard and seen, fantastic and strained as he felt it to be, possibly even the product of religious mania, was nevertheless profoundly disquieting, for mixed up with it somewhere or other was—truth. Mr. Skale *had* made a discovery—a giant one; it was not all merely talk and hypnotism, the glamour of words. His great Experiment would prove to be real and terrible. He *had* discovered certain uses of sound, occult yet scientific, and if he, Spinrobin, elected to stay on, he would be obliged to play his part in the dénouement. And this thought from the very beginning appalled while it fascinated him. It filled him with a kind of horrible amazement. For the object the clergyman sought, though not yet disclosed, already cast its monstrous shadow across his path. He somehow discerned that it would deal directly with knowledge the saner judgement of a commonplace world had always deemed undesirable, unlawful, unsafe, dangerous to the souls that dared attempt it, failure involving a pitiless and terrible Nemesis.

He lay in bed watching the play of the firelight upon the high ceiling, and thinking in confused fashion of the huge clergyman with his thundering voice, his great lambent eyes and his seductive gentleness; of his singular speculations and his hints, half menacing, half splendid, of things to come. Then he thought of the housekeeper with her deafness and her withered arm, and that white peace about her face; and, lastly, of Miriam, soft, pale beneath her dark skin, her gem-like eyes ever finding his own, and of the intimate personal relations so swiftly established between them...

It was, indeed, a singular household thus buried away in the heart of these lonely mountains. The stately old mansion was just the right setting for—for—

Unbidden into his mind a queer, new thought shot suddenly, interrupting the flow of ideas. He never understood how or whence it came, but with the picture of all the empty rooms in the corridor about him, he received the sharp unwelcome impression that when Mr. Skale described the house as empty it was really nothing of the sort. Utterly unannounced, the uneasy conviction took possession of him that the building was actually—populated. It was an extraordinary idea to have. There was absolutely nothing in the way of evidence to support it. And with it flashed across his memory echoes of that unusual catechism he had been subjected to—in particular the questions whether he believed in spirits,—"other life," as Skale termed it. Sinister suspicions flashed through his imagination as he lay there listening to the ashes dropping in the grate and watching the shadows cloak the room. Was it possible that there were occupants of these rooms that the man had somehow evoked from the interstellar spaces and crystallized by means of sound into form and shape—*created?*

Something freezing swept into him from a region far beyond the world. He shivered. These cold terrors that grip the soul suddenly without apparent cause, whence do they come? Why, out of these rather extravagant and baseless speculations, should have emerged this sense of throttling dread that appalled him? And why, once again, should he have felt convinced that the ultimate nature of the clergyman's great experiment was impious, fraught with a kind of heavenly danger, "unpermissible?"

Spinrobin, lying there shivering in his big bed, could not guess. He only knew that by way of relief his mind instinctively sought out Miriam, and so found peace. Curled up in a ball between the sheets his body presently slept, while his mind, intensely active, travelled off into that vast inner prairie of his childhood days and called her name aloud. And presumably she came to him at once, for his sleep was undisturbed and his dreams uncommonly sweet, and he woke thoroughly refreshed eight hours later, to find Mrs. Mawle standing beside his bed with thin bread and butter and a cup of steaming tea.

II

For the rest, the new secretary fell quickly and easily into the routine of this odd little household, for he had great powers of adaptability. At first the promise of excitement faded. The mornings were spent in the study of Hebrew, Mr. Skale taking great pains to instruct him in the vibratory pronunciation (for so he termed it) of certain words, and especially of the divine, or angelic, names. The correct utterance, involving a kind of prolonged and sonorous vibration of the vowels, appeared to be of supreme importance. He further taught him curious correspondences between Sound and Number, and the attribution to these again of certain colours. The vibrations of sound and light, as air and ether, had intrinsic importance, it seemed, in the uttering of certain names; all of which, however, Spinrobin learnt by rote, making neither head nor tail of it.

That there were definite results, though, he could not deny—psychic results; for a name uttered correctly produced one effect, and uttered wrongly produced another... just as a wrong note in a chord afflicts the hearer whereas the right one blesses...

The afternoons, wet or fine, they went for long walks together about the desolate hills, Miriam sometimes accompanying them. Their talk and laughter echoed all over the mountains, but there was no one to hear them, the nearest village being several miles away and the railway station—nothing but a railway station. The isolation was severe; there were no callers but the bi-weekly provision carts; letters had to be fetched and newspapers were neglected.

Arrayed in fluffy tweeds, with baggy knickerbockers and heavily-nailed boots, he trotted beside his giant companion over the moors, somewhat like a child who expected its hand to be taken over difficult places. His confidence had been completely won. The sense of shyness left him. He felt that he already stood to the visionary clergyman in a relationship that was more than secretarial. He still panted, but with enthusiasm instead of with regret. In the background loomed always the dim sense of the Discovery and Experiment approaching inevitably, just as in childhood the idea of Heaven and Hell had stood waiting to catch him—real only when he thought carefully about them. Skale was just the kind of man, he felt, who would make a discovery, so simple that the rest of the world had overlooked it, so tremendous that it struck at the roots of human knowledge. He had the simple originality of genius, and a good deal of its inspirational quality as well.

Before ten days had passed he was following him about like a dog, hanging upon his lightest word. New currents ran through him mentally and spiritually as the fires of Mr. Skale's vivid personality quickened his own, and the impetus of his inner life lifted him with its more violent momentum. The world of an ordinary man is so circumscribed, so conventionally moulded, that he can scarcely conceive of things that may dwell normally in the mind of an extraordinary man. Adumbrations of these, however, may throw their shadow across his field of vision. Spinrobin was ordinary in most ways, while Mr. Skale was un-ordinary in nearly all; and thus, living together in this intimate solitude, the secretary got peeps into his companion's region that gradually convinced him. With cleaned nerves and vision he began to think in ways and terms that were new to him. Skale, like some big figure in story or legend, moved forward into his life and waved a wand. His own smaller personality began to expand; thoughts entered unannounced that hitherto had not even knocked at the door, and the frontiers of his mind first wavered, then unfolded to admit them.

The clergyman's world, whether he himself were mad or sane, was a real world, alive, vibrating, shortly to produce practical results. Spinrobin would have staked his very life upon it...

And, meanwhile, he made love openly—under any other conditions, outrageously—to Miriam, whose figure of soft beauty moving silently about the house helped to redeem it. She rendered him quiet little services of her own accord that pleased him immensely, for occasionally he detected her delicate perfume about his room, and he was sure it was not Mrs. Mawle who put the fresh heather in the glass jars upon his table, or arranged his papers with such neat precision on the desk.

Her delicate, shining little face with its wreath of dark hair, went with him everywhere, hauntingly, possessingly; and when he kissed her, as he did now every morning and every evening under Mr. Skale's very eyes, it was like plunging his lips into a bed of wild flowers that no artificial process had ever touched. Something in him sang when she was near. She had, too, what he used to call as a boy "night eyes"—changing after dusk into such shadowy depths that to look *at* them was to look beyond and through them. The sight could never rest only upon their surface. Through her eyes, then, stretched all the delight of that old immense playground... where names clothed, described, and summoned living realities.

His attitude towards her was odd yet comprehensible; for though his desire was unquestionably great, it was not particularly active, probably because he knew that he held her and that no aggressive effort was necessary. Secure in the feeling that she belonged to him, and he to her, he also found that he had little enough to say to her, never anything to ask. She knew and understood it all beforehand; expression was uncalled for. As well might the brimming kettle sing to the water "I contain you," or the water reply "I fill you!"

Only this was not the simile he used. In his own thoughts from the very beginning he had used the analogy of sound—of the chord. As well might one note feel called upon to cry to another in the same chord, "Hark! I'm sounding with you!" as that Spinrobin should say to Miriam, "My heart responds and sings to yours."

After a period of separation, however, he became charged with things he wanted to say to her, all of which vanished utterly the moment they came together. Words instantly then became unnecessary, foolish. He heard that faint internal singing, and his own resonant response; and they merely stayed there side by side, completely happy, everything told without speech. This sense of blissful union enwrapped his soul. In the language of his boyhood he had found her name; he knew her; she was his.

Yet sometimes they did talk; and their conversations, in any other setting but this amazing one provided by the wizardry of Skale's enthusiasm, must have seemed exquisitely ludicrous. In the room, often with the clergyman a few feet away, reading by the fire, they would sit in the window niche, gazing into one another's eyes, perhaps even holding hands. Then, after a long interval of silence Mr. Skale would hear Spinrobin's thin accents:

"You brilliant little sound! I hear you everywhere within me, chanting a song of life!"

And Miriam's reply, thrilled and gentle:

"I'm but your perfect echo! My whole life sings with yours!"

Whereupon, kissing softly, they would separate, and Mr. Skale would cover them mentally with his blessing.

Sometimes, too, he would send for the housekeeper and, with the aid of the violin, would lead the four voices, his own bass included, through the changes of various chords, for the vibratory utterance of certain names; and the beauty of these sounds, singing the "divine names," would make the secretary swell to twice his normal value and importance (thus he puts it), as the forces awakened by the music poured and surged into the atmosphere about them. Whereupon the clergyman would explain with burning words that many a symphony of Beethoven's, a sonata of Schumann's, or a suite of Tschaikovsky's were the Names, peaceful, romantic or melancholy, of great spiritual Potencies, heard partially by these masters in their moments of inspirational ecstasy. The powers of these Beings were just as characteristic, their existence just as real, as the simpler names of the Hebrew angels, and their psychic influence upon the soul that heard them uttered just as sure and individual.

"For the power of music, my dear Spinrobin, has never yet by science or philosophy been adequately explained, and never can be until the occult nature of sound, and its correlations with colour, form, and number is once again understood. 'Rhythm is the first law of the physical creation,' says one, 'and music is a breaking into sound of the fundamental rhythm of universal being.' 'Rhythm and harmony,' declares Plato, 'find their way into the secret places of the soul.' 'It is the manifestation,' whispers the deaf Beethoven, 'of the inner essential nature of all that is,' or in the hint of Leibnitz, 'it is a calculation which the soul makes unconsciously in secret.' It is 'love in search of a name,' sang George Eliot, nearer in her intuition to the truth than all the philosophers, since love is the dynamic of pure spirit. But I," he continued after a pause for breath, and smiling amid the glow of his great enthusiasm, "go beyond and behind them all into the very heart of the secret; for you shall learn that to know the sounds of the Great Names and to utter their music correctly shall merge yourself into the heart of their deific natures and make you 'as the gods themselves…!'"

And Spinrobin, as he listened, noticed that a slight trembling ran across the fabric of his normal world, as though it were about to vanish and give place to another—a new world of divine things made utterly simple. For many things that Skale said in this easy natural way, he felt, were in the nature of clues and passwords, whose effect he carefully noted upon his secretary, being intended to urge him, with a certain violence even, into the desired region. Skale was testing him all the time.

III

And it was about this time, more than half way through the trial month, that the clergyman took Spinrobin, now become far more than merely secretary, into his fuller confidence. In a series of singular conversations, which the bewildered little fellow has reported to the best of his ability, he explained to him something of the science of true names. And to prove it he made two singular experiments: first he uttered the true name of Mrs. Mawle, secondly of Spinrobin himself, with results that shall presently be told.

These things it was necessary for him to know and understand before they made the great Experiment. Otherwise, if unprepared, he might witness results that would involve the loss of self-control and the failure, therefore, of the experiment—a disaster too formidable to contemplate.

By way of leading up to this, however, he gave him some account first of the original discovery. Spinrobin asked few questions, made few comments; he took notes, however, of all he heard and at night wrote them up as best he could in his diary. At times the clergyman rose and interrupted the strange recital by moving about the room with his soft and giant stride, talking even while his back was turned; and at times the astonished secretary wrote so furiously that he broke his pencil with a snap, and Mr. Skale had to wait while he sharpened it again. His inner excitement was so great that he almost felt he emitted sparks.

The clue, it appears, came to the clergyman by mere chance, though he admits his belief that the habits of asceticism and meditation he had practised for years may have made him in some way receptive to the vision, for as a vision, it seems, the thing first presented itself—a vision made possible by a moment of very rapid hypnosis.

An Anglican priest at the time, in charge of a small Norfolk parish, he was a great believer in the value of ceremonial—in the use, that is, of colour, odour and sound to induce mental states of worship and adoration—more especially, however, of sound as uttered by the voice, the human voice being unique among instruments in that it combined the characteristics of all other sounds. Intoning, therefore, was to him a matter of psychic importance, and it was one summer evening, intoning, in the chancel, that he noticed suddenly certain very curious results. The faces of two individuals in the congregation underwent a charming and singular change, a change which he would not describe more particularly at the moment, since Spinrobin should presently witness it for himself.

It all happened in a flash—in less than a second, and it is probable, he holds, that his own voice induced an instant of swift and passing hypnosis upon himself; for as he stood there at the lectern there came upon him a moment of keen interior lucidity in which he realized beyond doubt or question what had happened. The use of voice, bell, or gong, has long been known as a means of inducing the hypnotic state, and during this almost instantaneous trance of his there came a sudden revelation of the magical possibilities of sound-vibration. By some chance rhythm of his intoning voice he had hit upon the exact pitch, quality and accent which constituted the "Note" of more than one member of the congregation before him. Those particular individuals, without being aware of the fact, had at once responded, automatically and inevitably. For a second he had heard, he knew, their true names! He had unwittingly "called" them.

Spinrobin's heart leaped with excitement as he listened, for this idea of "Naming True" carried him back to the haunted days of his childhood clairvoyance when he had known Winky.

"I don't *quite* understand, Mr. Skale," he put in, desirous to hear a more detailed explanation.

"But presently you shall," was all the clergyman vouchsafed.

The clue thus provided by chance he had followed up, but by methods hard to describe apparently. A corner of the veil, momentarily lifted, had betrayed the value that lies in the repetition of certain sounds—the rhythmic reiteration of syllables—in a word, of chanting or incantation. By diving down into his subconscious region, already prepared by long spiritual training, he gradually succeeded in drawing out further details piece by piece, and finally by infinite practice and prayer welding them together into an intelligible system. The science of true-naming slowly, with the efforts of years, revealed itself. His mind slipped past the deceit of mere sensible appearances. Clair-audiently he heard the true inner names of things and persons...

Mr. Skale rose from his chair. With thumbs in the armholes of his waistcoat and fingers drumming loudly on his breast he stood over the secretary, who continued making frantic notes.

"That chance discovery, then, made during a moment's inner vision," he continued with a grave excitement, "gave me the key to a whole world of new knowledge, and since then I have made incredible developments. Listen closely, Mr. Spinrobin, while I explain. And take in what you can."

The secretary laid down his pencil and notebook. He sat forward in an attitude of intense eagerness upon the edge of his chair. He was trembling. This strange modern confirmation of his early Heaven of wonder before the senses had thickened and concealed it, laid bare again his earliest world of far-off pristine glory.

"The ordinary name of a person, understand then, is merely a sound attached to their physical appearance at birth by the parents—a meaningless sound. It is not their true name. That, however, exists behind it in the spiritual world, and is the accurate description of the soul. It is the sound you express visibly before me. The Word is the Life."

Spinrobin surreptitiously picked up his pencil; but the clergyman spied the movement. "Never mind the notes," he said; "listen closely to me." Spinrobin obeyed meekly.

"Your ordinary outer name, however," continued Mr. Skale, speaking with profound conviction, "may be made a conductor to your true, inner one. The connection between the two by a series of subtle interior links forms gradually with the years. For even the ordinary name, if you reflect a moment, becomes in time a sound of singular authority—inwoven with the finest threads of your psychical being, so that in a sense you *become* it. To hear it suddenly called aloud in the night—in a room full of people, in the street unexpectedly—is to know a shock, however small, of increased vitality. It touches the imagination. It calls upon the soul built up around it."

He paused a moment. His voice boomed musically about the room, even after he ceased speaking. Bewildered, wondering, delighted, Spinrobin drank in every word. How well he knew it all.

"Now," resumed the clergyman, lowering his tone unconsciously, "the first part of my discovery lies in this: that I have learned to pronounce the ordinary names of things and people in such a way as to lead me to their true, inner ones—"

"But," interrupted Spinrobin irrepressibly, "how in the name of—?"

"Hush!" cried Skale quickly. "Never again call upon a mighty name—in vain. It is dangerous. Concentrate your mind upon what I now tell you, and you shall understand a part, at least, of my discovery. As I was saying, I have learned how to find the true name by means of the false; and understand, if you can, that to pronounce a true name correctly means to participate in its very life, to vibrate with its essential nature, to learn the ultimate secret of its inmost being. For our true names are the sounds originally uttered by the 'Word' of God when He created us, or 'called' us into Being out of the void of infinite silence, and to repeat them correctly means literally—to—speak—with—His—Voice. It is to speak the truth." The clergyman dropped his tone to an awed whisper. "Words are the veils of Being; to speak them truly is to lift a corner of the veil."

"What a glory! What a thing!" exclaimed the other under his breath, trying to keep his mind steady, but losing control of language in the attempt. The great sentences seemed to change the little room into a temple where sacred things were about to reveal themselves. Spinrobin now understood in a measure why Mr. Skale's utterance of his own name and that of Miriam had sounded grand. Behind each he had touched the true name and made it echo.

The clergyman's voice brought his thoughts back from distances in that inner prairie of his youth where they had lost themselves.

"For all of us," he was repeating with rapt expression in his shining eyes, "are Sounds in the mighty music the universe sings to God, whose Voice it was that first produced us, and of whose awful resonance we are echoes therefore in harmony or disharmony." A look of power passed into his great visage. Spinrobin's imagination, in spite of the efforts that he made, fluttered with broken wings behind the swift words. A flash of the former terror stirred in the depths of him. The man was at the heels of knowledge it is not safe for humanity to seek...

"Yes," he continued, directing his gaze again upon the other, "that is a part of my discovery, though only a part, mind. By repeating your outer name in a certain way until it disappears in the mind, I can arrive at the real name within. And to utter it is to call upon the secret soul—to summon it from its lair. 'I have redeemed thee; I have called thee by name.' You remember the texts? '*I know thee by name,*' said Jehovah to the great Hebrew magician, '*and thou art mine.*' By certain rhythms and vibratory modulations of the voice it is possible to produce harmonics of sound which awaken the inner name into life—and then to spell it out. Note well, to *spell* it,—spell—incantation—the magical use of sound—the meaning of the Word of Power, used with such terrific effect in the old forgotten Hebrew magic. Utter correctly the names of their Forces, or Angels, I am teaching you daily now," he went on reverently, with glowing eyes and intense conviction; "pronounce them with full vibratory power that awakens all their harmonics, and you awaken also their counterpart in yourself; you summon their strength or characteristic quality to your aid; you introduce their powers actively into your own psychical being. Had Jacob succeeded in discovering the 'Name' of that 'Angel' with whom he wrestled, he would have become one with its superior power and have thus conquered it. Only, he asked instead of commanded, and he found it not..."

"Magnificent! Splendid!" cried Spinrobin, starting from his chair, seizing with his imagination potently stirred, this possibility of developing character and rousing the forces of the soul.

"We shall yet call upon the Names, and see," replied Skale, placing a great hand upon his companion's shoulder, "not aloud necessarily, but by an inner effort of intense will which sets in vibration the finer harmonics heard only by the poet and magician, those harmonics and overtones which embody the psychical element in music. For the methods of poet and magician, I tell you, my dear Spinrobin, are identical, and all the faiths of the world are at the heels of that thought. Provided you have faith you can—move mountains! You can call upon the very gods!"

"A most wonderful idea, Mr. Skale," faltered the other breathlessly, "quite wonderful!" The huge sentences deafened him a little with their mental thunder.

"And utterly simple," was the reply, "for all truth is simple."

He paced the floor like a great caged animal. He went down and leaned against the dark bookcase, with his legs wide apart, and hands in his coat pockets. "To name truly, you see, is to evoke, to create!" he roared from the end of the room. "To utter as it should be uttered any one of the Ten Words, or Creative Powers of the Deity in the old Hebrew system, is to become master of the 'world' to which it corresponds. For these names are still in living contact with the realities behind. It means to vibrate with the powers that called the universe into being and—into form."

A sort of shadowy majesty draped his huge figure, Spinrobin thought, as he stood in semi-darkness at the end of the room and thundered forth these extraordinary sentences with a conviction that, for the moment at least, swept away all doubt in the mind of his listener. Dreadful ideas, huge-footed and threatening, rushed to and fro in the secretary's mind. He was torn away from all known anchorage, staggered, dizzy and dismayed; yet at the same time, owing to his adventure-loving temperament, a prey to some secret and delightful exaltation of the spirit. He was out of his depth in great waters...

Then, quite suddenly, Mr. Skale came swiftly over to his side and whispered in accents that were soothing in comparison:

"And think for a moment how beautiful, the huge Words by which God called into being the worlds, and sent the perfect, rounded bodies of the spheres spinning and singing, blazing their eternal trails of glory through the void! How sweet the whisper that crystallized in flowers! How tender the note that fashioned the eyes and face, say, of Miriam..."

At the name of Miriam he felt caught up and glorified, in some delightful and inexplicable way that brought with it—peace. The power of all these strange and glowing thoughts poured their full tide into his own rather arid and thirsty world, frightening him with their terrific force. But the mere utterance of that delightful name—in the way Skale uttered it—brought confidence and peace.

"... Could we but hear them!" Skale continued, half to himself, half to his probationer; "for the sad thing is that today the world has ears yet cannot hear. As light is distorted by passing through a gross atmosphere, so sound reaches us but indistinctly now, and few true names can bring their wondrous messages of power correctly. Men, coarsening with the materialism of the ages, have grown thick and gross with the luxury of inventions and the diseases of modern life that develop intellect at the expense of soul. They have lost the old inner hearing of divine sound, and but one here and there can still catch the faint, far-off and ineffable music."

He lifted his eyes, and his voice became low and even gentle as the glowing words fell from his heart of longing.

"None hear now the morning stars when they sing together to the sun; none know the chanting of the spheres! The ears of the world are stopped with lust, and the old divine science of true-naming seems lost forever amid the crash of engines and the noisy thunder of machinery!... Only among flowers and certain gems are the accurate old true names still to be found!... But we are on the track, my dear Spinrobin, we are on the ancient trail to Power."

The clergyman closed his eyes and clasped his hands, lifting his face upwards with a rapt expression while he murmured under his breath the description of the Rider on the White Horse from the Book of the Revelations, as though it held some inner meaning that his heart knew yet dared not divulge: "And he had a Name written, that no man knew but he himself. And he was clothed in a vesture dipped in blood: and his Name is called The Word of God... and he hath on his vesture and on his thigh a name written,—'King of Kings and Lord of Lords...'"

And for an instant Spinrobin, listening to the rolling sound but not to the actual words, fancied that a faintly coloured atmosphere of deep scarlet accompanied the vibrations of his resonant whisper and produced in the depths of his mind this momentary effect of coloured audition.

It was all very strange and puzzling. He tried, however, to keep an open mind and struggle as best he might with these big swells that rolled into his little pool of life and threatened to merge it in a vaster tide than he had yet dreamed of. Knowing how limited is the world which the senses report, he saw nothing too inconceivable in the idea that certain persons might possess a peculiar inner structure of the spirit by which supersensuous things can be perceived. And what more likely than that a man of Mr. Skale's unusual calibre should belong to them? Indeed, that the clergyman possessed certain practical powers of an extraordinary description he was as certain as that the house was not empty as he had at first supposed. Of neither had he proof as yet; but proof was not long in forthcoming.

I

"Then if there is so much sound about in all objects and forms—if the whole universe, in fact, is sounding," asked Spinrobin with a naïve impertinence not intended, but due to the reaction of his simple mind from all this vague splendour, "why don't we hear it more?"

Mr. Skale came upon him like a boomerang from the end of the room. He was smiling. He approved the question.

"With us the question of hearing is merely the question of wavelengths in the air," he replied; "the lowest audible sound having a wavelength of sixteen feet, the highest less than an inch. Some people can't hear the squeak of a bat, others the rumble of an earthquake. I merely affirm that in every form sleeps the creative sound that is its life and being. The ear is a miserable organ at best, and the majority are far too gross to know clair-audience. What about sounds, for instance, that have a wavelength of a hundred, a thousand miles on the one hand, or a millionth part of an inch on the other?"

"A thousand miles! A millionth of an inch?" gasped the other, gazing at his interlocutor as though he was some great archangel of sound.

"Sound for most of us lies between, say, thirty and many thousand vibrations per second—the cry of the earthquake and the cricket; it is our limitation that renders the voice of the dewdrop and the voice of the planet alike inaudible. We even mistake a measure of noise—like a continuous millwheel or a river, say—for silence, when in reality there is no such thing as perfect silence. Other life is all the time singing and thundering about us," he added, holding up a giant finger as though to listen. "To the imperfection of our ears you may ascribe the fact that we do not hear the morning stars shouting together."

"Thank you, yes, I quite see now," said the secretary. "To name truly is to hear truly." The clergyman's words seemed to hold a lamp to a vast interior map in his mind that was growing light. A new dawn was breaking over the great mental prairie where he wandered as a child. "To find the true name of anything," he added, "you mean, is to hear its sound, its individual note as it were?" Incredible perspectives swam into his ken, hitherto undreamed of.

"Not 'as it were,'" boomed the other. "You *do* hear it. After which the next step is to utter it, and so absorb its force into your own being by synchronous vibration—union mystical and actual. Only, you must be sure you utter it correctly. To pronounce incorrectly is to call it incompletely into life and form—to distort and injure it, and yourself with it. To make it untrue—a lie."

They were standing in the dusk by the library window, watching the veil of night that slowly covered the hills. The flying horizons of the moors had slipped away into the darkness.

The stars were whispering together their thoughts of flame and speed. At the back of the room sat Miriam among the shadows, like some melody hovering in a musician's mind till he should call her forth. It was close upon the tea hour. Behind them Mrs. Mawle was busying herself with lamps and fire. Mr. Skale, turning at the sound of the housekeeper, motioned to the secretary to approach, then stooped down and spoke low in his ear:

"With many names I had great difficulty," he whispered. "With hers, for instance," indicating the housekeeper behind them. "It took me five years' continuous research to establish her general voice-outline, and even then I at first only derived a portion of her name. And in uttering it I made such errors of omission and pronunciation that her physical form suffered, and she emerged from the ordeal in disorder. You have, of course, noticed her disabilities... But, later, though only in stammering fashion, I called upon her all complete, and she has since known a serene blessedness and a sense of her great value in the music of life that she never knew before." His face lit up as he spoke of it. "For in that moment she found herself. She heard her true name, God's creative sound, thunder through her being."

Spinrobin, feeling the clergyman's forces pouring through him like a tide at such close proximity, bowed his head. His lips were too dry to frame words. He was thinking of the possible effects upon his own soul and body when his name too should be "uttered." He remembered the withered arm and the deafness. He thought, too, of that slender, ghostly figure that haunted the house with its soft movements and tender singing. Lastly, he remembered his strange conviction that somewhere in the great building, possibly in his own corridor, there were other occupants, other life, Beings of unearthly scale waiting the given moment to appear, summoned by utterance.

"And you will understand now why it is I want a man of high courage to help me," Skale resumed in a louder tone, standing sharply upright; "a man careless of physical existence, and with a faith wholly beyond the things of this world!"

"I do indeed," he managed to reply aloud, while in his thoughts he was saying, "I will, I *must* see it through. I won't give in!" With all his might he resisted the invading tide of terror. Even if sad results came later, it was something to have been sacrificed in so big a conception.

In his excitement he slipped from the edge of the windowsill, where he was perched, and Mr. Skale, standing close in front of him, caught his two wrists and set him upon his feet. A shock, like a rush of electricity, ran through him. He took his courage boldly in both hands and asked the question ever burning at the back of his mind.

"Then, this great Experiment you—we have in view," he stammered, "is to do with the correct uttering of the names of some of the great Forces, or Angels, and—and the assimilating of their powers into ourselves—?"

Skale rose up gigantically beside him. "No, sir," he cried, "it is greater—infinitely greater than that. Names of mere Angels I can call alone without the help of any one; but for the name I wish to utter a whole chord is necessary even to compass the utterance of the opening syllable; as I have told you already, a chord in which you share the incalculable privilege of being the tenor note. But for the completed syllables—the full name—!" He closed his eyes and shrugged his massive shoulders—"I may need the massed orchestras of half the world, the chorused voices of the entire nation—or in their place a still small voice of utter purity crying in the wilderness! In time you shall know fully—know, see and hear. For the present, hold your soul with what patience and courage you may."

The words thundered about the room, so that Miriam, too, heard them. Spinrobin trembled inwardly, as though a cold air passed him. The suggestion of immense possibilities, vague yet terrible, overwhelmed him again suddenly. Had not the girl at that moment moved up beside him and put her exquisite pale face over his shoulder, with her hand upon his arm, it is probable he would then and there have informed Mr. Skale that he withdrew from the whole affair.

"Whatever happens," murmured Miriam, gazing into his eyes, "we go on singing and sounding together, you and I." Then, as Spinrobin bent down and kissed her hair, Mr. Skale put an arm round each of them and drew them over to the tea table.

"Come, Mr. Spinrobin," he said, with his winning smile, "you must not be alarmed, you know. You must not desert me. You are necessary to us all, and when my Experiment is complete we shall all be as gods together. Do not falter. There is nothing in life, remember, but to lose oneself; and I have found a better way of doing so than any one else—by merging ourselves into the Voice of—"

"Mr. Skale's tea has been standing more than ten minutes," interrupted the old housekeeper, coming up behind them; "if Mr. Spinrobin will please to let him come—" as though it was Spinrobin's fault that there had been delay.

Mr. Skale laughed good-humouredly, as the two men, suddenly in the region of teacups and buttered toast, looked one another in the face with a certain confusion. Miriam, sipping her tea, laughed too, curiously. Spinrobin felt restored to some measure of safety and sanity again. Only the strange emotion of a few moments before still moved there unseen among them.

"Listen, and you shall presently hear her name," the clergyman whispered, glancing up at the other over his teacup, but Spinrobin was crunching his toast too noisily to notice the meaning of the words fully.

II

The Stage Manager who stands behind all the scenes of life, both great and small, had prepared the scene well for what was to follow. The sentences about the world of inaudible sound had dropped the right kind of suggestion into the secretary's heart. His mind still whirred with a litter of half-digested sentences and ideas, however, and he was vividly haunted by the actuality of truth behind them all. His whole inner being at that moment cried "Hark!" through a hush of expectant wonder.

There they sat at tea, this singular group of human beings: Mr. Skale, bigger than ever in his loose housesuit of black, swallowing his liquid with noisy gulps; Spinrobin, nibbling slippery morsels of hot toast, on the edge of his chair; Miriam, quiet and mysterious, in her corner; and Mrs. Mawle, sedate, respectful in cap and apron, presiding over the teapot, the whole scene cosily lit by lamp and fire—when this remarkable new thing happened. Spinrobin declares always that it came upon him like a drowning wave, frightening him not with any idea of injury to himself, but with a dreadful sense of being lost and shelterless among the immensities of a transcendent new world. Something passed into the room that made his soul shake and flutter at the centre.

His attention was first roused by a sound that he took, perhaps, to be the wind coming down from the hills in those draughts and gusts he sometimes heard, only to his imagination now it was a peopled wind crying round the walls, behind whose voice he detected the great fluid form of it—running and coloured. But, with the noise, a terror that was no ordinary terror invaded the recesses of his soul. It was the fear of the Unknown, dreadfully multiplied.

He glanced up quickly from his teacup, and chancing to meet Miriam's eye, he saw that she was smiling as she watched him. This sound, then, had some special significance. At the same instant he perceived that it was not outside but in the room, close beside him, that Mr. Skale, in fact, was talking to the deaf housekeeper in a low and carefully modulated tone—a tone she could not possibly have heard, however. Then he discovered that the clergyman was not speaking actually, but repeating her name. He was intoning it. It grew into a kind of singing chant, an incantation.

"Sarah Mawle... Sarah Mawle... Sarah Mawle..." ran through the room like water. And, in Skale's mouth, it sounded as his own name had sounded—different. It became in some significant way—thus Spinrobin expresses it always—stately, important, nay, even august. It became real. The syllables led his ear away from their normal signification—away from the outer toward the inner. His ordinary mental picture of the mere letters SARAHMAWLE disappeared and became merged in something else—into something alive that pulsed and moved with vibrations of its own. For, with the outer sound there grew up another interior one, that finally became separate and distinct.

Now Spinrobin was well aware that the continued repetition of one's own name can induce self-hypnotism; and he also knew that the reiteration of the name of an object ends by making that object disappear from the mind. "Mustard," repeated indefinitely, comes to have no meaning at all. The mind drops behind the mere symbol of the sound into something that is unintelligible, if not meaningless. But here it was altogether another matter, and from the torrent of words and similes he uses to describe it, this—a curious mixture of vividness and confusion—is apparently what he witnessed:

For, as the clergyman's resonant voice continued quietly to utter the name, something passed gradually into the appearance of the motherly old housekeeper that certainly was not there before, not visible, at least, to the secretary's eyes. Behind the fleshly covering of the body, within the very skin and bones it seemed, there flowed with steady splendour an effect of charging new vitality that had an air of radiating from her face and figure with the glow and rush of increased life. A suggestion of grandeur, genuine and convincing, began to express itself through the humble domestic exterior of her everyday self; at first, as though some greater personage towered shadowy behind her, but presently with a growing definiteness that showed it to be herself and nothing separate. The two, if two they were, merged.

Her mien, he saw, first softened astonishingly, then grew firm with an aspect of dignity that was unbelievably beautiful. An air of peace and joy her face had always possessed, but this was something beyond either. It was something imposing, majestic. So perilously adjusted is the ludicrous to the sublime, that while the secretary wondered dumbly whether the word "housekeeper" might also in Skale's new world connote "angel," he could have laughed aloud, had not the nobility of the spectacle hinted at the same time that he should have wept. For the tears of a positive worship started to his eyes at the sight.

"Sarahmawle... Sarahmawle..." The name continued to pour itself about him in a steady ripple, neither rising nor falling, and certainly not audible to those deaf old ears that flanked the vigorous and unwrinkled face. "Youth" is not the word to describe this appearance of ardent intensity that flamed out of the form and features of the housekeeper, for it was something utterly apart from either youth or age. Nor was it any mere idealization of her worn and crumpled self. It was independent of physical conditions, as it was independent of the limitations of time and space; superb as sunshine, simple as the glory that had sometimes touched his soul of boyhood in sleep—the white fires of an utter transfiguration.

It was, in a word, as if the name Skale uttered had summoned to the front, through all disguising barriers of flesh, her true and naked spirit, that which neither ages nor dies, that which the eyes, when they rest upon a human countenance, can never see—the Soul itself!

For the first time in his life Spinrobin, abashed and trembling, gazed upon something in human guise that was genuinely sublime—perfect with a stainless purity. The mere sight produced in him an exaltation of the spirit such as he had never before experienced... swallowing up his first terror. In his heart of hearts, he declares, he prayed; for this was the natural expression for an emotion of the volume and intensity that surged within him...

How long he sat there gazing seems uncertain; perhaps minutes, perhaps seconds only. The sense of time's passage was temporarily annihilated. It might well have been a thousand years, for the sight somehow swept him into eternity... In that tearoom of Skale's lonely house among the mountains, the warmth of an earthly fire upon his back, the light of an earthly oil-lamp in his eyes, holding buttered toast in exceedingly earthly fingers, he sat face to face with something that yet was not of this earth, something majestic, spiritual and eternal... visible evidence of transfiguration and of "earth growing heaven..."

It was, of course, stupid and clumsy of Spinrobin to drop his teacup and let it smash noisily against the leg of the table; yet it was natural enough, for in his ecstasy and amazement he apparently lost control of certain muscles in his trembling fingers... Though the change came gradually it seemed very quick. The volume of the clergyman's voice grew less, and as the tide of sound ebbed the countenance of the housekeeper also slowly altered. The flames that a moment before had burned so whitely there flickered faintly and were gone; the glory faded; the splendour withdrew. She even seemed to dwindle in size... She resumed her normal appearance. Skale's voice ceased.

The incident apparently had occupied but a few moments, for Mrs. Mawle, he realized, was gathering the plates together and fitting them into the spaces of the crowded tea-tray with difficulty—an operation, he remembered, she had just begun when the clergyman first began to call upon her name.

She, clearly, had been conscious of nothing unusual. A moment later, with her customary combination of curtsey and bow, she was gone from the room, and Spinrobin, acting upon a strange impulse, found himself standing upright by the table, looking wildly about him, passing his hand through his scattered hair, and trying in vain to utter words that should relieve his overcharged soul of the burden of glory and mystery that oppressed it.

A pain, profoundly searching, pierced his heart. He thought of the splendours he had just witnessed, and of the joy and peace upon those features even when the greater wonder withdrew. He thought of the power in the countenance of Skale, and of the shining loveliness in the face of Miriam. Then, with a blast of bitterest disappointment, he realized the insignificance of his own self—the earthiness of his own personality, the dead, dull ordinariness of his own appearance. Why, oh, why, could not all faces let the soul shine through? Why could not all identify themselves with their eternal part, and thus learn happiness and joy? A sense of the futile agony of life led him with an impassioned eagerness again to the thought of Skale's tremendous visions, and of the great Experiment that beckoned beyond. Only, once more the terror of its possible meaning dropped upon him, and the little black serpents of fear shot warningly across this brighter background of his hopes.

Then he was aware that Miriam had crossed the room and stood beside him, for her delicate and natural perfume announced her even before he turned and saw. Her soft eyes shining conveyed an irresistible appeal, and with her came the sense of peace she always brought. She was the one thing at that moment that could comfort and he opened his arms to her and let her come nestling in against him, both hands finding their way up under the lapels of his coat, all the exquisite confidence of the innocent child in her look. Her hair came over his lips and face like flowers, but he did not kiss her, nor could he find any words to say. To hold her there was enough, for the touch of her healed and blessed him.

"So now you have seen her as she really is," he heard her voice against his shoulder; "you have heard her true name, and seen a little of its form and colour!"

"I never guessed that in this world—" he stammered; then, instead of completing the sentence, held her more tightly to him and let his face sink deeper into the garden of her hair.

"Oh yes," she answered, and then peered up with unflinching look into his eyes, "for that is just how I see you too—bright, splendid and eternal."

"Miriam!" It was as unexpected as a ghost and as incredible. "Me...?"

"Of course! You see I know your true name. I see you as you are within!"

Something came to steady his swimming brain, but it was only after a distinct effort that he realized it was the voice of Mr. Skale addressing him. Then, gradually, as he listened, gently releasing the girl in order to turn towards him, he understood that what he had witnessed had been in the nature of a "test"—one of those tests he had been warned would come—and that his attitude to it was regarded by the clergyman with approval.

"It was a test more subtle than you know, perhaps, Mr. Spinrobin," he was saying, "and the feelings it has roused in you are an adequate proof that you have come well through it. As I knew you would, as I knew you would," he added, with evident satisfaction. "They do infinite credit both to yourself and to our judgement in—er—accepting you."

A wave of singular emotion seemed to pass across the room from one to the other that, catching the breathless secretary in its tide, filled him with a high pride that he had been weighed and found worthy, then left him cold with a sudden reaction as he realized after some delay the import of the words Mr. Skale was next saying to him.

CH·5

"And now you shall hear your own name called," boomed the clergyman with enthusiasm, "and realize the beauty and importance of your own note in the music of life."

And while Spinrobin trembled from head to toe Mr. Skale bore down upon him and laid a hand upon his shoulder. He looked up into the clergyman's luminous eyes. His glance next wandered down the ridge of that masterful nose and lost itself among the flowing strands of the tangled beard. At that moment it would hardly have surprised him to see the big visage disappear, and to hear the Sound, of which it was the visible form, slip into his ears with a roar.

But side by side with the vague terror of the unknown he was conscious also of a smaller and more personal pang. For a man may envy other forms, yet keenly resent the possible loss or alteration of his own. And he remembered the withered arm and the deafness.

"But," he faltered, yet ashamed of his want of courage, "I don't want to lose my present shape, or—come back—without—"

"Have no fear," exclaimed the other with decision. "Miriam and myself have not been experimenting in vain these three weeks. We have found your name. We know it accurately. For we are all one chord, and as I promised you, there is no risk." He stopped, lowering his voice; and, taking the secretary by the arm with a fatherly and possessive gesture, "Spinrobin," he whispered solemnly, "you shall learn the value and splendour of your Self in the melody of the Universe—that burst of divine music! You shall understand how closely linked you are to myself and Mrs. Mawle, but, closest of all, to Miriam. For Miriam herself shall call your name, and you shall hear!"

So little Miriam was to prove his executioner, or his redeemer. That was somehow another matter. The awe with which these experiments of Mr. Skale's inspired him ebbed considerably as he turned and saw the appealing, wistful expression of his other examiner. Brave as a lion he felt, yet timid as a hare; there was no idea of real resistance in him any longer.

"I'm ready, then," he said faintly, and the girl came up softly to his side and sought his face with a frank innocence of gaze that made no attempt to hide her eagerness and joy. She accepted the duty with delight, proudly conscious of its importance.

"I know thee by name and thou art mine," she murmured, taking his hand.

"It makes me happy, yet afraid," he replied in her ear, returning the caress; and at that moment the clergyman who had gone to fetch his violin, returned into the room with a suddenness that made them both start—for the first time. Very slightly, with the first sign of that modesty which comes with knowledge he had yet noticed in her, or felt conscious of in himself, she withdrew, a wonderful flush tinging her pale skin, then passing instantly away.

"To make you feel absolutely safe from possible disaster," Mr. Skale was saying with a smile, "you shall have the assistance of the violin. The pitch and rhythm shall be thus assured. There is nothing to fear."

And Miriam, equally smiling with confidence, led her friend, perplexed and entangled as he was by the whole dreamlike and confusing puzzle—led him to the armchair she had just vacated, and then seated herself at his feet upon a high footstool and stared into his eyes with a sweet and irresistible directness of gaze that at once increased both his sense of bewilderment and his confidence.

"First, you must speak my name," she said gently, yet with a note of authority, "so that I may get the note of your voice into myself. Once or twice will do."

He obeyed. "Miriam... Miriam... Miriam," he said, and watched the tiny reflection of his own face in her eyes, her "night-eyes." The same moment he began to lose himself. The girl's lips were moving. She had picked up his voice and merged her own with it, so that when he ceased speaking her tones took up the note continuously. There was no break. She carried on the sound that he had started.

And at the same moment, out of the corner of his eye, he perceived that the violin had left its case and was under the clergyman's beard. The bow undulated like a silver snake, drawing forth long, low notes that flowed about the room and set the air into rhythmical vibrations. These vibrations, too, carried on the same sound. Spinrobin gave a little uncontrollable jump; he felt as if he had uttered his own death-warrant and that this instrument proclaimed the sentence. Then the feeling of dread lessened as he heard Mr. Skale's voice mingling with the violin, combining exquisitely with the double-stopping he was playing on the two lower strings; for the music, as the saying is, "went through him" with thrills of power that plunged into unknown depths of his soul and lifted him with a delightful sense of inner expansion to a state where fear was merged in joy.

For some minutes the voice of Miriam, murmuring so close before him that he could feel her very breath, was caught in the greater volume of the violin and bass. Then, suddenly, both Skale and violin ceased together, and he heard her voice emerge alone. With a little rush like that of a singing flame, it dropped down on to the syllables of his name—his ugly and ridiculous outer and ordinary name:

"ROBERTSPINROBIN... ROBERTSPINROBIN..." he heard; and the sound flowed and poured about his ears like the murmur of a stream through summer fields. And, almost immediately, with it there came over him a sense of profound peace and security. Very soon, too, he lost the sound itself—did not hear it, as sound, for it grew too vast and enveloping. The sight of Miriam's face also he lost. He grew too close to her to see her, as object. Both hearing and sight merged into something more intimate than either. He and the girl were together—one consciousness, yet two aspects of that one consciousness.

They were two notes singing together in the same chord, and he had lost his little personality, only to find it again, increased and redeemed, in an existence that was larger.

It seemed to Spinrobin—for there is only his limited phraseology to draw from—that the incantation of her singing tones inserted itself between the particles of his flesh and separated them, ran with his blood, covered his skin with velvet, flowed and purred in the very texture of his mind and thoughts. Something in him swam, melted, fused. His inner kingdom became most gloriously extended...

His soul loosened, then began to soar, while something at the heart of him that had hitherto been congealed now turned fluid and alive. He was light as air, swift as fire. His thoughts, too, underwent a change: rose and fell with the larger rhythm of new life as the sound played upon them, somewhat as wind may rouse the leaves of a tree, or call upon the surface of a deep sea to follow it in waves. Terror was nowhere in his sensations; but wonder, beauty and delight ran calling to one another from one wave to the next, as this tide of sound moved potently in the depths of his awakening higher consciousness. The little reactions of ordinary life spun away from him into nothingness as he listened to a volume of sound that was oceanic in power and of an infinite splendour: the creative sound by which God first called him into form and being—the true inner name of his soul.

... Yet he no longer consciously listened... no longer, perhaps, consciously heard. The name of the soul can sound only in the soul, where no speech is, nor any need for such stammering symbols. Spinrobin for the first time knew his true name, and that was enough.

It is impossible to translate into precise language this torrent of exquisite sensation that the girl's voice awakened. In the secret chambers of his imagination Spinrobin found the *thoughts*, perhaps, that clothed it with intelligible description for himself, but in speaking of it to others he becomes simply semi-hysterical, and talks a kind of hearty nonsense. For the truth probably is that only poetry or music can convey any portion of a mystical illumination, otherwise hopelessly incommunicable. The outer name had acted as a conductor to the inner name beyond. It filled the room, and filled some far vaster space that opened out above the room, about the house, above the earth, yet at the same time was deep, deep down within his own self. He passed beyond the confines of the world into those sweet, haunted gardens where Cherubim and Seraphim—vast Forces—continually do sing. It floated him off his feet as a rising tide overtakes the little shore-pools and floats them into its own greatness, and on the tranquil bosom of these giant swells he rose into a state that was too calm to be ecstasy, yet too glorious to be mere exaltation.

And as his own little note of personal aspiration soared with this vaster music to which it belonged, he felt mounting out of himself into a condition where at last he was alive, complete and splendidly important. His sense of insignificance fled. His ordinary petty and unvalued self dropped away flake by flake, and he realized something of the essential majesty of his own real Being as part of an eternal and wonderful Whole. The little painful throb of his own limited personality slipped into the giant pulse-beat of a universal vibration.

In his normal daily life, of course, he lost sight of this Whole, blinded by the details seen without perspective, mistaking his little personality for all there was of him; but now, as he rose, whirling, soaring, singing in the body of this stupendous music, he understood with a rush of indescribable glory that he was part and parcel of this great chord—this particular chord in which Skale, Mrs. Mawle and Miriam also sang their harmonious existences—that this chord, again, was part of a vaster music still, and that all, in the last resort, was a single note in the divine Utterance of God.

That is, the little secretary, for the first time in his existence, saw life as a whole, and interpreted the vision so wondrous sweet and simple, with the analogies of sound communicated to his subliminal mind by the mighty Skale. Whatever the cause, however, the fine thing was that he saw, heard, knew. He was of value in the scheme. In future he could pipe his little lay without despair.

Moreover, with a merciless clarity of vision, he perceived an even deeper side of truth, and understood that the temporary discords were necessary, just as evil, so-called, is necessary for the greater final perfection of the Whole. For it came to him with the clear simplicity of a child's vision that the process of attuning his being to the right note must inevitably involve suffering and pain: the awful stretching of the string, the strain of the lifting vibrations, the stress at first of sounding in harmony with all the others, and the apparent loss of one's own little note in order to do so...

This point he reached, it seems, and grasped. Afterwards, however, he entered a state where he heard things no man can utter because no language can touch transcendental things without confining or destroying them. In attempting a version of them he merely becomes unintelligible, as has been said. Yet the mere memory of it brings tears to his blue eyes when he tries to speak of it, and Miriam, who became, of course, his chief confidant, invariably took it upon herself to stop his futile efforts with a kiss.

So at length the tide of sound began to ebb, the volume lessened and grew distant, and he found himself, regretfully, abruptly, sinking back into what by comparison was mere noise. First, he became conscious that he listened—heard—saw; then, that Miriam's voice still uttered his name softly, but his ordinary, outer name, Robertspinrobin; that he noticed her big grey eyes gazing into his own, and her lips moving to frame the syllables, and, finally, that he was sitting in the armchair, trembling. Joy, peace, wonder still coursed through him like flames, but dying flames. Mr. Skale's voice next reached him from the end of the room. He saw the fireplace, his own bright and pointed pumps, the tea table where they had drunk tea, and then, as the clergyman strode towards him over the carpet, he looked up, faint with the farewell of the awful excitement, into his face. The great passion of the experience still glowed and shone in him like a furnace.

And there, in that masterful bearded visage, he surprised an expression so tender, so winning, so comprehending, that Spinrobin rose to his feet, and taking Miriam by the hand, went to meet him. There the three of them stood upon the mat before the fire. He felt overwhelmingly drawn to the personality of the man who had revealed to him such splendid things, and in his mind stirred a keen and poignant regret that such knowledge could not be permanent and universal, instead of merely a heavenly dream in the mind of each separate percipient. Gratitude and love, unknown to him before, rose in his soul. Spinrobin, his heart bursting as with flames, had cried aloud, "You have called me by my name and I am free!... You have named me truly and I am redeemed!..." And all manner of speech, semi-inspirational, was about to follow, when Mr. Skale suddenly moved to one side and raised his arm. He pointed to the mirror.

Spinrobin was just tall enough to see his own face in the glass, but the glimpse he caught made him stand instantly on tiptoe to see more. For his round little countenance, flushed as it was beneath its fringe of disordered feathery hair, was literally—transfigured. A glory, similar to the glory he had seen that same evening upon the face of the housekeeper, still shone and flickered about the eyes and forehead. The signature of the soul, brilliant in purity, lay there, transforming the insignificance of the features with the grandeur and nobility of its own power.

"I am honoured,—too gloriously honoured!" was the singular cry that escaped his lips, vainly seeking words to express an emotion of the unknown, "I am honoured as the sun... and as the stars...!"

And so fierce was the tide of emotion that rose within him at the sight, so strong the sense of gratitude to the man and girl who had shown him how his true Self might contain so great a glory, that he turned with a cry like that of a child bewildered by the loss of some incomprehensible happiness—turned and flung himself first upon the breast of the big clergyman, and then into the open arms of the radiant Miriam, with sobs and tears of wonder that absolutely refused to be restrained.

I

The situation at this point of his amazing adventure seems to have been that the fear Spinrobin felt about the nature of the final Experiment was met and equalized by his passionate curiosity regarding it. Had these been the only two forces at work, the lightest pressure in either direction would have brought him to a decision. He would have accepted the challenge and stayed; or he would have hesitated, shirked, and left.

There was, however, another force at work upon which he had hardly calculated at the beginning, and that force now came into full operation and controlled his decision with margin and to spare. He loved Miriam; and even had he not loved her, it is probable that her own calm courage would have put him to shame and made him "face the music." He could no more have deserted her than he could have deserted himself. The die was cast.

Moreover, if the certainty that Mr. Skale was trafficking in dangerous and unlawful knowledge was formidable enough to terrify him, for Miriam, at least, it held nothing alarming. She had no qualms, knew no uneasiness. She looked forward to the end with calmness, even with joy, just as ordinary good folk look forward to a heaven beyond death. For she had never known any other ideal. Mr. Skale to her was father, mother and God. He had brought her up during all the twenty years of her life in this solitude among the mountains, choosing her reading, providing her companionship, training her with the one end in view of carrying out his immense and fire-stealing purpose.

She had never dreamed of any other end, and had been so drilled with the idea that this life was but a tedious training-place for a worthier state to come, that she looked forward, naturally enough, with confidence and relief to the great Experiment that should bring her release. She knew vaguely that there was a certain awful danger involved, but it never for one instant occurred to her that Mr. Skale could fail. And, so far, Spinrobin had let no breath of his own terror reach her, or attempted ever to put into her calm mind the least suggestion that the experiment might fail and call down upon them the implacable and destructive forces that could ruin them body and soul forever. For this, plainly expressed, was the form in which his terror attacked him when he thought about it. Skale was tempting the Olympian powers to crush him.

It was about this time, however, as has been seen from a slight incident in the last chapter, that a change began to steal, at first imperceptibly, then obviously, over their relations together. Spinrobin had been in the house three weeks—far longer, no doubt, than any of the other candidates. There only remained now the final big tests. The preliminary ones were successfully passed. Miriam knew that very soon the moment would come for him to stay—or go. And it was in all probability this reflection that helped her to make certain discoveries in herself that at first she did not in the least understand.

Spinrobin, however, understood perfectly. His own heart made him intuitive enough for that. And the first signs thrilled and moved him prodigiously. His account of it all is like no love story that has ever been heard, for in the first place this singular girl hardly breathed about her the reality of an actual world. She had known nothing beyond the simple life in this hollow of the hills on the one hand, and on the other the portentous conceptions that peopled the region of dream revealed by the clergyman. And in the second place she had no standards but her own instincts to judge by, for Mrs. Mawle, in spite of her devotion to the girl, suffered under too great disabilities to fill the place of a mother, while Mr. Skale was too lost in his vast speculations to guide her except in a few general matters, and too sure of her at the same time to reflect that she might ever need detailed guidance. Her exceedingly natural and wholesome bringing-up on the one hand, and her own native purity and good sense on the other, however, led her fairly straight; while the fact that Spinrobin, with his modesty and his fine aspirations, was a "little gentleman" into the bargain, ensured that no unlawful temptation should be placed in her way, or undue pressure, based upon her ignorance, employed.

II

They were coming down one afternoon from the mountains soon after the test of calling his name, and they were alone, the clergyman being engaged upon some mysterious business that had kept him out of sight all day. They did not talk much, but they were happy in each other's company, Spinrobin more than happy. Much of the time, when the ground allowed, they went along hand in hand like children.

"Miriam," he had asked on the top of the moors, "did I ever tell you about Winky—my little friend Winky?" And she had looked up with a smile and shaken her head. "But I like the name," she added; "I should like to hear, please." And he told her how as a boy he had invoked various folk to tease his sister, of whom Winky was chief, but in telling the story he somehow or other always referred to the little person by name, and never once revealed his sex. He told, too, how he sat all night on the lawn outside his sister's window to intercept the expected visit.

"Winky," she said, speaking rather low, "is a true name, of course. You really created Winky—called Winky into being." For to her now this seemed as true and possible as it had seemed to himself at the age of ten.

"Oh, I really loved Winky," he replied enthusiastically, and was at the same moment surprised to feel her draw away her hand. "Winky lived for years in my very heart."

And the next thing he knew, after a brief silence between them, was that he heard a sob, and no attempt to smother it either. In less than a second he was beside her and had both her hands in his. He understood in a flash.

"You precious baby," he cried, "but Winky was a little man. He wasn't a girl!"

She looked up through her tears—oh, but how wonderful her grey eyes were through tears!—and made him stand still before her and repeat his sentence. And she said, "I know it's true, but I like to hear you say it, and that's why I asked you to repeat it."

"Miriam," he said to her softly, kneeling down on the heather at her feet, "there's only one name in my heart, I can tell you that. I heard it sing and sing the moment I came into this house, the very instant I first saw you in that dark passage. I knew perfectly well, ages and ages ago, that one day a girl with your name would come singing into my life to make me complete and happy, but I never believed that she would look as beautiful as you are." He kissed the two hands he held. "Or that she—would—would think of me as you do," he stammered in his passion.

And then Miriam, smiling down on him through her tears, bent and kissed his feathery hair, and immediately after was on her knees in front of him among the heather.

"I own you," she said quite simply. "I know your name, and you know mine. Whatever happens—" But Spinrobin was too happy to hear any more, and putting both arms round her neck, he kissed the rest of her words away into silence.

And in the very middle of this it was that the girl gently, but very firmly, pushed him from her, and Spinrobin in the delicacy of his mind understood that for the first time in her curious, buried life the primitive instincts had awakened, so that she knew herself a woman, and a woman, moreover, who loved.

Thus caught in a bewildering network of curiosity, fear, wonder, and—love, Spinrobin stayed on, and decided further that should the clergyman approve him he would not leave. Yet his intimate relations now with Miriam, instead of making it easier for him to learn the facts, made it on the other hand more difficult. For he could not, of course, make use of her affection to learn secrets that Mr. Skale did not yet wish him to know. And, further, he had no desire to be disloyal either to him. None the less he was sorely tempted to ask her what the final experiment was, and what the "empty" rooms contained. And most of all what the great name was they were finally to utter by means of the human chord.

The emotions playing about him at this time, however, were too complicated and too violent to enable him to form a proper judgement of the whole affair. It seems, indeed, that this calmer adjudication never came to him at all, for even to this day the mere mention of the clergyman's name brings to his round cheeks a flush of that enthusiasm and wonder which are the enemies of all sober discrimination. Skale still remains the great battering force of his life that carried him off his feet towards the stars, and sent his imagination with wings of fire tearing through the Unknown to a goal that once attained should make them all four as gods.

I

And thus the affair moved nearer to its close. The theory and practice of moulding form by means of sound was the next bang at his mind—delivered in the clergyman's most convincing manner, and, in view of the proofs that soon followed, an experience that seemed to dislocate the very foundations of his visible world, deemed hitherto secure enough at least to stand on.

Had it all consisted merely of talk on Mr. Skale's part the secretary would have known better what to think. It was the interludes of practical proof that sent his judgement so awry. These definite, sensible results, sandwiched in between all the visionary explanation, left him utterly at sea. He could not reconcile them altogether with hypnotism. He could only, as an ordinary man, already with a bias in the mystical direction, come to the one conclusion that this overwhelming and hierophantic man was actually in touch with cisterns of force so terrific as to be dangerous to what he had hitherto understood to be—life. It was easy enough for the clergyman, in his optimistic enthusiasm, to talk about their leading to a larger life. But what if the experiment failed, and these colossal powers ran amok upon the world—and upon the invokers?

Moreover—chief anxiety of all—what was this name to be experimented with? What was the nature of this force that Skale hoped to invoke—so mighty that it should make them "as gods," so terrible that a chord alone could compass even the first of its stupendous syllables?

And, further, he was still haunted with the feeling that other "beings" occupied certain portions of the rambling mansion, and more than once recently he had wakened in the night with an idea, carried over from dreams possibly, that the corridor outside his bedroom was moving and alive with footsteps. "From dreams possibly," for when he went and peered shivering through the narrow crack of the half-opened door, he saw nothing unusual. And another time—he was awake beyond question at the moment, for he had been reading till two o'clock and had but just extinguished the candle—he had heard a sound that he found impossible to describe, but that sent all the blood with a swift rush from the region of his heart. It was not wind; it was not the wood cracking with the frost; it was not snow sliding from the slates outside. It was something that simultaneously filled the entire building, yet sounded particularly loud just outside his door; and it came with the abrupt suddenness of a report. It made him think of all the air in the rooms and halls and passages being withdrawn by immense suction, as though a gigantic dome had been dropped over the building in order to produce a vacuum. And just after it he heard, unmistakably, the long soft stride of Skale going past his door and down the whole length of the corridor—stealthily, very quickly, with the hurry of anxiety or alarm in his silence and his speed.

This, moreover, had now happened twice, so that imagination seemed a far-fetched explanation. And on both occasions the clergyman had remained invisible on the day following until the evening, and had then reappeared, quiet and as usual, but with an atmosphere of immense vibratory force somehow about his person, and a glow in his face and eyes that at moments seemed positively coloured.

No word of explanation, however, had as yet been forthcoming of these omens, and Spinrobin waited with what patience he could, meanwhile, for the final test which he knew to be close upon him. And in his diary, the pages usually left blank now because words failed him, he wrote a portion of Oenone's cry that had caught his memory and expressed a little of what he felt:

> ... for fiery thoughts
> Do shape themselves within me, more and more,
> Whereof I catch the issue, as I hear
> Dead sounds at night come from the inmost hills,
> *Like footsteps upon wool...*

II

It was within three days of the expiration of his trial month that he then had this conversation with the clergyman, which he understood quite well was offered by way of preparation for the bigger tests about to come. He has reported what he could of it; it seemed to him at the time both plausible and absurd; it was of a piece, that is, with the rest of the whole fabulous adventure.

Mr. Skale, as they walked over the snowy moors in the semi-darkness between tea and dinner, had been speaking to him about the practical results obtainable by sound-vibrations (what he already knew for that matter), and how it is possible by fiddling long enough upon a certain note to fiddle down a bridge and split it asunder. From that he passed on to the scientific fact that the ultimate molecules of matter are not only in constant whirring motion, but that also they do not actually touch one another. The atoms composing the point of a pin, for instance, shift and change without ceasing, and—there is space between them.

Then, suddenly taking Spinrobin's arm, he came closer, his booming tone dropping to a whisper:

"To change the form of anything," he said in his ear, "is merely to change the arrangement of those dancing molecules, to alter their rate of vibration." His eyes, even in the obscurity of the dusk, went across the other's face like flames.

"By means of sound?" asked the other, already beginning to feel eerie.

The clergyman nodded his great head in acquiescence.

"Just as the vibrations of heat-waves," he said after a pause, "can alter the form of a metal by melting it, so the vibrations of sound can alter the form of a thing by inserting themselves between those whirling molecules and changing their speed and arrangement—change the outline, that is."

The idea seemed fairly to buffet the little secretary in the face, but Mr. Skale's proximity was too overpowering to permit of very clear thinking. Feeling that a remark was expected from him, he managed to ejaculate an obvious objection in his mind.

"But is there any sound that can produce vibrations fine and rapid enough—to—er—accomplish such a result?"

Mr. Skale appeared almost to leap for pleasure as he heard it. In reality he merely straightened himself up.

"That," he cried aloud, to the further astonishment and even alarm of his companion, "is another part of my discovery—an essential particular of it: the production of sound-vibrations fine and rapid enough to alter shapes! Listen and I will tell you!" He lowered his voice again. "I have found out that by uttering the true inner name of anything I can set in motion harmonics—harmonics, note well, half the wave length and twice the frequency!—that are delicate and swift enough to insert themselves between the whirling molecules of any reasonable object—any object, I mean, not too closely or coherently packed. By then swelling or lowering my voice I can alter the scale, size or shape of that object almost indefinitely, its parts nevertheless retaining their normal relative proportions. I can scatter it to a huge scale by separating its molecules indefinitely, or bring them so closely together that the size of the object would be reduced to a practical invisibility!"

"Recreate the world, in fact!" gasped Spinrobin, feeling the earth he knew slipping away under his feet.

Mr. Skale turned upon him and stood still a moment. The huge moors, glimmering pale and unreal beneath their snow, ran past them into the sky—silent forms corresponding to who knows what pedal notes? The wind sighed—audible expression of who shall say what mighty shapes?... Something of the passion of sound, with all its mystery and splendour, entered his heart in that windy sigh. Was anything real? Was anything permanent?... Were Sound and Form merely interchangeable symbols of some deeper uncatalogued Reality? And was the visible cohesion after all the illusory thing?

"Re-mould the whole universe, sir!" he roared through the darkness, in a way that made the other wish for the touch of Miriam's hand to steady him. "I could make you, my dear Spinrobin, immense, tiny, invisible, or by a partial utterance of your name, permanently crooked. I could overwhelm your own vibrations and withdraw their force, as by suction of a vacuum, absorbing yourself into my own being. By uttering the name of this old earth, if I knew it, I could alter its face, toss the forests like green dust into the sea, and lift the pebbles of the seashore to the magnitude of moons! Or, did I know the true name of the sun, I could utter it in such a way as to identify myself with its very being, and so escape the pitiful terrors of a limited personal existence!"

He seized his companion's arm and began to stride down the mountainside at a terrific pace, almost lifting Spinrobin from his feet as he did so. About the ears of the panting secretary the wild words tore like bullets, whistling a new and dreadful music.

"My dear fellow," he shouted through the night, "at the Word of Power of a true man the nations would rush into war, or sink suddenly into eternal peace; the mountains be moved into the sea, and the dead arise. To know the sounds behind the manifestations of Nature, the names of mechanical as well as of psychical Forces, of Hebrew angels, as of Christian virtues, is to know Powers that you can call upon at will—and use! Utter them in the true vibratory way and you waken their counterpart in yourself and stir thus mighty psychic powers into activity in your Soul."

He rained the words down upon the other's head like a tempest.

"Can you wonder that the walls of Jericho fell flat before a 'Sound,' or that the raging waves of the sea lay still before a voice that called their Name? My discovery, Mr. Spinrobin, will run through the world like a purifying fire. For to utter the true names of individuals, families, tribes and nations, will be to call them to the knowledge of their highest Selves, and to lift them into tune with the music of the Voice of God."

They reached the front door, where the gleam of lamps shone with a homely welcome through the glass panels. The clergyman released his companion's arm; then bent down towards him and added in a tone that held in it for the first time something of the gravity of death:

"Only remember—that to utter falsely, to pronounce incorrectly, to call a name incompletely, is the beginning of all evil. For it is to lie with the very soul. It is also to evoke forces without the adequate corresponding shape that covers and controls them, and to attract upon yourself the destructive qualities of these Powers—to your own final disintegration and annihilation."

Spinrobin entered the house, filled with a sense of awe that was cold and terrible, and greater than all his other sensations combined. The winds of fear and ruin blew shrill about his naked soul. None the less he was steadfast. He would remain to bless. Mr. Skale might be violent in mind, unbalanced, possibly mad; but his madness thundered at the doors of heaven, and the sound of that thundering completed the conquest of his admiration. He really believed that when the end came those mighty doors would actually open. And the thought woke a kind of elemental terror in him that was not of this world—yet marvellously attractive.

III

That night the singular rushing sound again disturbed him. It seemed as before to pass through the entire building, but this time it included a greater space in its operations, for he fancied he could hear it outside the house as well, travelling far up into the recesses of the dark mountains. Like the sweep of immense draughts of air it went down the passage and rolled on into the sky, making him think of the clergyman's suggestion that some sounds might require airwaves of a hundred miles instead of a few inches, too vast to be heard as sound. And shortly after it followed the great gliding stride of Mr. Skale himself down the corridor. That, at least, was unmistakable.

During the following day, moreover, Mr. Skale remained invisible. Spinrobin, of course, had never permitted himself to search the house, or even to examine the other rooms in his own corridor. The quarters where Miriam slept were equally unknown to him. But he was quite certain that these prolonged periods of absence were spent by the clergyman in some remote part of the rambling building where there existed isolated, if not actually secret, rooms in which he practised the rituals of some dangerous and intrepid worship. And these intimidating and mysterious sounds at night were, of course, something to do with the forces he conjured...

The day was still and windless, the house silent as the grave. He walked about the hills during the afternoon, practising his Hebrew "Names" and "Words" like a schoolboy learning a lesson. And all about him the slopes of mountain watched him, listening. So did the sheet of snow, shining in the wintry sunlight. The clergyman seemed to have put all sound in his pocket and taken it away with him. The absence of anything approaching noise became almost oppressive. It was a Silence that prepares. Spinrobin went about on tiptoe, spoke to Miriam in whispers, practised his Names in hushed, expectant tones. He almost expected to see the moors and mountains open their deep sides and let the Sounds of which they were the visible shape escape awfully about him...

In these hours of solitude, all that Skale had told him, and more still that he divined himself, haunted him with a sense of disquieting reality. Inaudible sounds of fearful volume, invisible forms of monstrous character, combinations of both even, impended everywhere about him. He became afraid lest he might stumble, as Skale had done, on the very note that should release them and bring them howling, leaping, crashing about his ears. Therefore, he tried to make himself as small as possible; he muffled steps and voice and personality. If he could, he would have completely disappeared.

He looked forward to Skale's return, but when evening came he was still alone, and he dined *tête-à-tête* with Miriam for the first time. And she, too, he noticed, was unusually quiet. Almost they seemed to have entered the world of Mrs. Mawle, the silent regions of the deaf. But for the most part it is probable that these queer impressions were due to the unusual state of Spinrobin's imagination. He knew that it was his last night in the place—unless the clergyman accepted him; he knew also that Mr. Skale had absented himself with a purpose, and that the said purpose had to do with the test of Alteration of Forms by Sound, which would surely be upon him before the sun rose.

So that, one way and another, it was natural enough that his nerves should have been somewhat overtaxed.

The presence of Miriam and Mrs. Mawle, however, did much to soothe him. The latter, indeed, mothered the pair of them quite absurdly, smiling all the time while she moved about softly with the dishes, and doing her best to make them eat enough for four. Between courses she sat at the end of the room, waiting in the shadows till Miriam beckoned to her, and once or twice going so far as to put her hand upon Spinrobin's shoulder protectively.

His own mind, however, all the time was full of charging visions. He kept thinking of the month just past and of the amazing changes it had brought into his thoughts. He realized, too, now that Mr. Skale was away, something of the lonely and splendid courage of the man, following this terrific, perhaps mad, ideal, day in day out, week in week out, for twenty years and more, his faith never weakening, his belief undaunted. Waves of pity, too, invaded him for the first time—pity for this sweet girl, brought up in ignorance of any other possible world; pity for the deaf old housekeeper, already partially broken, and both sacrificed to the dominant idea of this single, heaven-climbing enthusiast; pity last of all for himself, swept headlong before he had time to reflect, into the audacious purpose of this violent and headstrong super-man.

All manner of emotions stirred now this last evening in his perplexed breast; yet out of the general turmoil one stood forth more clearly than the rest—his proud consciousness that he was taking an important part in something really big at last. Behind the screen of thought and emotion which veiled so puzzlingly the truth, he divined for the first time in his career a golden splendour. If it also terrified him, that was only his cowardice... In the same way it might be splendid to jump into Niagara just above the falls to snatch a passing flower that seemed more wonderful than any he had seen before, but—!

"Miriam, tomorrow is my last day," he said suddenly, catching her grey eyes upon him in the middle of his strange reflections. "Tonight may be my last night in this house with you."

The girl made no reply, merely looking up and smiling at him. But the singing sensation that usually accompanied her gaze was not present.

"That was very nearly—a discord," she observed presently, referring to his remark. "It was out of tune!" And he realized with a touch of shame what she meant. For it was not true that this was his last evening; he knew really that he would stay on and that Mr. Skale would accept him. Quick as a flash, with her simple intuition, she felt that he had said this merely to coax from her some sign of sympathy or love. And the girl was not to be drawn. She knew quite well that she held him and that their fate, whatever it might be, lay together.

The gentle rebuke made him silent again. They sat there smiling at one another across the table, and old Mrs. Mawle, sitting among the shadows at the far end of the room, her hands crossed in front of her, her white evening cap shining like a halo above her patient face, watched them, also smiling. The rest of the strange meal passed without conversation, for the great silence that all day had wrapped the hills seemed to have invaded the house as well and laid its spell upon every room. A deep hush, listening and expectant, dropped more and more about the building and about themselves.

After dinner they sat for twenty minutes together before the library fire, their toes upon the fender, for, contrary to her habit, Miriam had not vanished at once to her own quarters.

"We're not alone here," remarked Spinrobin presently, in a low voice, and she nodded her head to signify agreement. The presence of Mr. Skale when he was in the house but invisible, was often more real and tremendous than when he stood beside them and thundered. Some part of him, some emanation, some potent psychic messenger from his personality, kept them closely company, and tonight the secretary felt it very vividly. His remark was really another effort to keep in close touch with Miriam, even in thought. He needed her more than ever in this sea of silence that was gathering everywhere about him. Gulf upon gulf it rose and folded over him. His anxiety became every moment more acute, and those black serpents of fear that he dreaded were not very far away. By every fibre in his being he felt certain that a test which should shake the very foundations of his psychical life was slowly and remorselessly approaching him.

Yet, though he longed to speak outright and demand of Miriam what she knew, and especially that she should reveal the place of the clergyman's concealment and what portent it was that required all this dread and muted atmosphere for its preparation, he kept a seal upon his lips, realizing that loyalty forbade, and that the knowledge of her contempt would be even worse than the knowledge of the truth.

And so in due course she rose to go, and as he opened the door for her into the hall, she paused a moment and turned towards him. A sudden inexplicable thrill flashed through him as she turned her eyes upon his face, for he thought at first she was about to speak. He has never forgotten the picture as she stood there so close to his side, the lamplight on her slim figure in its white silk blouse and neat dark skirt, the gloom of the unlit hall and staircase beyond—stood there an instant, then put both her arms about his neck, drew him down to her, and kissed him gently on both cheeks. Twice she kissed him, then was gone into the darkness, so softly that he scarcely heard her steps, and he stood between the shadows and the light, her perfume still lingering, and with it the sweet and magical blessing that she left behind. For that caress, he understood, was the innocent childlike caress of their first days, and with all the power of her loving little soul in it she had given him the message that he craved: "Courage! And keep a brave heart, dear Spinny, *tonight*!"

I

Spinrobin lingered a while in the library after Miriam was gone, then feeling slightly ill at ease in the room now that her presence was withdrawn, put the lights out, saw that the windows were properly barred and fastened, and went into the hall on his way to bed.

He looked at the front door, tried the chain, and made sure that both top and bottom bolts were thrown. Why he should have taken these somewhat unusual precautions was not far to seek, though at the moment he could not probably have explained. The desire for protection was awake in his being, and he took these measures of security and defence because it sought to express itself, as it were, even automatically. Spinrobin was afraid.

Up the broad staircase he went softly with his lighted candle, leaving the great hall behind him full to the brim with shadows—shadows that moved and took shape. His own head and shoulders in monstrous outline poured over the walls and upper landings, and thence leaped to the skylight overhead. As he passed the turn in the stairs, the dark contents of the hall below rushed past in a single mass, like an immense extended wing, and settled abruptly at his back, following him thence to the landing.

Once there, he went more quickly, moving on tiptoe, and so reached his own room halfway down. He passed two doors to get there; another two lay beyond; all four, as he believed, being always locked. It was these four rooms that conjured mightily with his imagination always, for these were the rooms he pictured to himself, though without a vestige of proof, as being occupied. It was from the further ones—one or other of them—he believed Mr. Skale came when he had passed down the corridor at two in the morning, stealthily, hurriedly, on the heels of that rush of sound that made him shake in his bed as he heard it.

In his own room, however, surrounded by the familiar and personal objects that reminded him of normal life, he felt more at home. He undressed quickly, all his candles alight, and then sat before the fire in the armchair to read a little before getting into bed.

And he read for choice Hebrew—Hebrew poetry, and on this particular occasion, the books of Job and Ezekiel. For nothing had so soothing and calming an effect upon him as the mighty yet simple imagery of these sonorous stanzas; they invariably took him "out of himself," or at any rate out of the region of small personal alarms. And thus, letting his fancy roam, it seems, he was delighted to find that gradually the fears which had dominated him during the day and evening disappeared. He passed with the poetry into that region of high adventure which his nature in real life denied him. The verses uplifted him in a way that made his recent timidity seem the mere mood of a moment, or at least negligible. His memory, as one thing suggested another, began to give up its dead, and some of Blake's drawings, seen recently in London with prodigious effect, began to pass vividly before his mental vision.

The symbolism of what he was reading doubtless suggested the memory. He felt himself caught in the great invisible nets of wonder that forever swept the world. The littleness of modern life, compared to that ancient and profound spirit which sought the permanent things of the soul, haunted him with curious insistence. He suffered a keen, though somewhat mixed realization of his actual insignificance, yet of his potential sublimity could he but identify himself with his ultimate Self in the region of vision... His soul was aware of finding itself alternately ruffled and exalted as he read... and pondered... as he visualized to some degree the giant Splendours, the wonderful Wheels, the spirit Wings and Faces and all the other symbols of potent imagery evoked by the imagination of that old Hebrew world...

So that when, an hour later, pacified and sleepy, he rose to go to bed, this poetry seems to have left a very marked effect upon his mind—mingled, naturally enough, with the thought of Mr. Skale. For on his way across the floor, having adjusted the fire-screen, he distinctly remembered thinking what a splendid "study" the clergyman would have made for one of Blake's representations of the Deity—the flowing beard, the great nose, the imposing head and shoulders, the potentialities of the massive striding figure, surrounded by a pictorial suggestion of all the sound-forces he was forever talking about...

This thought was his last, and it was without fear of any kind. Merely, he insists, that his imagination was touched, and in a manner perfectly accountable, considering the ingredients of its contents at the time.

And so he hopped nimbly into bed. On the little table beside him stood the candle and the copy of the Hebrew text he had been reading, with its parallel columns in the two languages. His Jaeger slippers were beneath the chair, his clothes, carefully folded, on the sofa, his collar, studs and necktie in a row on the top of the mahogany chest of drawers. On the mantelpiece stood the glass jar of heather, filled that very day by Miriam. He saw it just as he blew out the candle, and Miriam, accordingly, was the last vision that journeyed with him into the country of dreams and sweet forgetfulness.

The night was perfectly still. Winter, black and hard, lay about the house like an iron wall. No wind stirred. Snow covered the world of mountain and moor outside, and Silence, supreme at midnight, poured all her softest forces upon the ancient building and its occupants. Spinrobin, curled up in the middle of the big four-poster, slept like a tired baby.

II

It was a good deal later when somewhere out of that mass of silence rose the faint beginnings of a sound that stirred first cautiously about the very foundations of the house, and then, mounting inch by inch, through the hall, up the staircase, along the corridor, reached the floor where the secretary slept so peacefully, and finally entered his room. Its muffled tide poured most softly over all. At first only this murmur was audible, as of "footsteps upon wool," of wind or drifting snow, a mere ghost of sound; but gradually it grew, though still gentle and subdued, until it filled the space from ceiling unto floor, pressing in like water dripping into a cistern with ever-deepening note as its volume increased. The trembling of air in a big belfry where bells have been a-ringing represents best the effect, only it was a trifle sharper in quality—keener, more alive.

But, also, there was something more in it—something gong-like and metallic, yet at the same time oddly and suspiciously human. It held a temper, too, that somehow woke the "panic sense," as does the hurried note of a drum—some quick emotional timbre that stirs the sleeping outposts of apprehension and alarm. On the other hand, it was constant, neither rising nor falling, and thus ordinarily, it need not have stirred any emotion at all—least of all the emotion of consternation. Yet, there was that in it which struck at the root of security and life. It was a revolutionary sound.

And as it took possession of the room, covering everything with its garment of vibration, it slipped in also, so to speak, between the crevices of the sleeping, unprotected Spinrobin, colouring his dreams—his innocent dreams—with the suggestion of nightmare dread. Of course, he was too deeply wrapped in slumber to receive the faintest intimation of this waking analysis. Otherwise he might, perhaps, have recognized the kind of primitive, ancestral dread his remote forefathers knew when the inexplicable horror of a tidal wave or an eclipse of the sun overwhelmed them with the threatened alteration of their entire known universe.

The sleeping figure in that big four-poster moved a little as the tide of sound played upon it, fidgeting this way and that. The human ball uncoiled, lengthened, straightened out. The head, half hidden by folds of sheet and pillowcase, emerged.

Spinrobin unfolded, then opened his eyes and stared about him, bewildered, in the darkness.

"Who's there? Is that you—anybody?" he asked in a whisper, the confusion of sleep still about him.

His voice seemed dead and smothered, as though the other sound overwhelmed it. The same instant, more widely awake, he realized that his bedroom was *humming*.

"What's that? What's the matter?" he whispered again, wondering uneasily at the noise.

There was no answer. The vague dread transferred itself adroitly from his dream-consciousness to his now thoroughly awakened mind. It began to dawn upon him that something was wrong. He noticed that the fire was out, and the room dark and heavy. He realized dimly the passage of time—a considerable interval of time—and that he must have been asleep several hours. Where was he? *Who* was he? What, in the name of mystery and night, had been going on during the interval? He began to shake all over—feverishly. Whence came this noise that made everything in the darkness tremble?

As he fumbled hurriedly for the matchbox, his fingers caught in the folds of pillowcase and sheet, and he struggled violently to get them clear again. It was while doing this that the impression first reached him that the room was no longer quite the same. It had changed while he slept. Even in the darkness he felt this, and shuddering pulled the blankets over his head and shoulders, for this idea of the changed room plucked at the centre of his heart, where terror lay waiting to leap out upon him.

After what seemed five minutes he found the matchbox and struck a light, and all the time the torrent of sound poured about his ears with such an effect of bewilderment that he hardly realized what he was doing. A strange terror poured into him that *he* would change with the room. At length the match flared, and while he lit the candle with shaking fingers, he looked wildly, quickly about him. At once the sounds rushed upon him from all directions, burying him, so to speak, beneath vehement vibrations of the air that rained in upon him... Yes, the room had indeed changed, actually changed... but before he could decide where the difference lay the candle died down to a mere spark, waiting for the wick to absorb the grease. It seemed like half an hour before the yellow tongue grew again, so that he finally saw clearly.

But—saw what? Saw that the room had horribly altered while he slept, yes! But how altered? What in the name of all the world's deities was the matter with it? The torrent of sound, now growing louder and louder, so confused him at first, and the dancing patchwork of light and shadow the candle threw so increased his bewilderment, that for some minutes he sought in vain to steady his mind to the point of accurate observation.

"God of my Fathers!" cried Spinrobin at last under his breath, and hardly knowing what he said, "if it's not moving!"

For this, indeed, was what he saw while the candle flame burned steadily upon a room that was no longer quite recognizable.

At first, with the natural exaggeration due to shock, he thought the whole room moved, but as his powers of sight came with time to report more truly, he perceived that this was only true of certain things in it. It was not the ceiling that poured down in fluid form to meet a floor ever gliding and shifting forward into outlandish proportions, but it was certain objects—one here, another there—midway between the two that, having assumed new and unaccustomed outlines, lent to the rest of the chamber a general appearance of movement and an entirely altered expression. And these objects, he perceived, holding tightly to the bedclothes with both hands as he stared, were two: the dark, old-fashioned cupboard on his left, and the plush curtains that draped the window on his right. He himself, and the bed and the rest of the furniture were stationary. The room as a whole stood still, while these two common and familiar articles of household furnishing took on a form and an expression utterly foreign to what he had always known as a cupboard and a curtain. This outline, this expression, moreover, if not actually sinister, was grotesque to the verge of the sinister: monstrous.

The difficulty of making any accurate observation at all was further increased by the perplexity of having to observe two objects, not even on the same side of the room. Their outlines, however, Spinrobin claims, altered very slowly, wavering like the distorted reflections seen in moving water, and unquestionably obeying in some way the pitch and volume of the sound that continued to pour its resonant tide about the room. The sound manipulated the shape; the connection between the two was evident. That, at least, he grasped. Somebody hidden elsewhere in the house—Mr. Skale probably, of course, in one of his secret chambers—was experimenting with the "true names" of these two "common objects," altering their normal forms by inserting the vibrations of sound between their ultimate molecules.

Only, this simple statement that his clearing mind made to itself in no way accounted for the fascination of horror that accompanied the manifestation. For he recognized it as the joy of horror and not alone the torment. His blood ran swiftly to the rhythm of these humming vibrations that filled the space about him; and his terror, his bewilderment, his curious sense of elation seemed to him as messengers of far more terrific sensations that communicated to him dimly the rushing wonder of some aspect of the Unknown in its ultimate nature essentially beautiful.

This, however, only dawned upon him later, when the experiment was complete and he had time to reflect upon it all next day; for, meanwhile, to see the proportions he had known since childhood alter thus before his eyes was unbelievably dreadful. To see your friend sufficiently himself still to be recognizable, yet in essentials, at the same time, grotesquely altered, would doubtless touch a climax of distress and horror for you. The changing of these two things, so homely and well-known in themselves, into something that was not themselves, involved an idea of destruction that was worse than even death, for it meant that the idea in the mind no longer corresponded to the visible object there before the eyes. The correspondence was no longer a true one. The result was a lie.

To describe the actual forms assumed by these shifting and wavering bodies is not possible, for when Spinrobin gives the details one simply fails to recognize either cupboard or curtain. To say that the dark, lumbering cupboard, standing normally against the wall down there in the shadows, loomed suddenly forward and upward, bent, twisted, and stretched out the whole of one side towards him like a misshapen arm, can convey nothing of the world of new sensations that the little secretary felt while actually watching it in progress in that haunted chamber of Skale's mansion among the hills. Nor can one be thrilled with the extraordinary sense of wonder that thrilled

Spinrobin when he saw the faded plush curtain hang across the window in such a way that it might well have wrapped the whole of Wales into a single fold, yet without extending its skirts beyond the actual walls of the room. For what he saw apparently involved contradictions in words, and the fact is that no description of what he saw is really possible at all.

"Hark! By thunder!" he exclaimed, creeping out of bed with sheer stress of excitement, while the sounds poured up through the floor as though from cellars and tunnels where they lay stored beneath the house. They sang and trembled about him with the menaces of a really exquisite alarm. He moved cautiously out into the centre of the room, not daring to approach too close to the affected objects, yet furiously anxious to discover how it was all done. For he was uncommonly "game" through it all, and had himself well in hand from beginning to end. He was really too excited, probably, to feel ordinary fear; it all swept him away too mightily for that; he did not even notice the sting of the hot candle-grease as it fell upon his bare feet.

There he stood, plucky little Spinny, steady amid this shifting world, master of his soul amid dissolution, his hair pointing out like ruffled feathers, his blue eyes wide open and charged with a speechless wonder, his face pale as chalk, lips apart, jaw a trifle dropped, one hand in the pocket of his dressing-gown, and the other holding the candle at an angle that showered grease upon the carpet of the Rev. Philip Skale as well as upon his own ankles. There he stood, face to face with the grotesque horror of familiar outlines gone wrong, the altered panorama of his known world moving about him in a strange riot of sound and form. It was, he understood, an amazing exhibition of the transforming power of sound—of sound playing tricks with the impermanence and the illusion of Form. Skale was making his words good.

And behind the scenes he divined, with a shudder of genuine admiration, the figure of the master of the ceremonies, somehow or other grown colossal, as he had thought of him just before going to sleep—Philip Skale, hidden in the secret places of the building, directing the operations of this dreadful aspect of his revolutionary Discovery... And yet the thought brought a measure of comfort in its train, for was he not also himself now included in the mighty scheme?... In his mind he saw this giant Skale, with his great limbs and shoulders, his flowing, shaggy beard, his voice of thunder and his portentous speculations, and, so doing, felt himself merged in a larger world that made his own little terrors and anxieties of but small account. Once again the sense of his own insignificance disappeared as he realized that at last he was in the full flood of an adventure that was providing the kind of escape he had always longed for.

Inevitably, then, his thought flew to Miriam, and as he remembered her final word to him a few short hours ago in the hall below, he already felt ashamed of the fear with which he had met the beginning of the "test." He instantly felt steeped instead in the wonder and power of the whole thing. His mind, though still trembling and shaken, came to rest. He drew, that is, upon the larger powers of the Chord.

And the interesting thing was that the moment this happened he noticed a change begin to come over the room. With extraordinary swiftness the tide of vibration lessened and the sound withdrew; the humming seemed to sink back into the depths of the house; the thrill and delight of his recent terrors fled with it. The air gradually ceased to shake and tremble; the furniture, with a curious final shiver as of spinning coins about to settle, resumed its normal shape. Once more the room, and with it the world, became commonplace and dull. The test apparently was over. He had met it with success.

Spinrobin, holding the candle straight for the first time, turned back towards the bed. He caught a passing glimpse of himself in the mirror as he went—white and scattered he describes his appearance... He climbed again into bed, blew the candle out, put the matchbox under his pillow within easy reach, and so once more curled himself up into a ball and composed himself to sleep.

I

But he was hardly settled—there had not even been time to warm the sheets again—when he was aware that the test, instead of being over, was, indeed, but just beginning; and the detail that conveyed this unwelcome knowledge to him, though small enough in itself, was yet fraught with a crowded cargo of new alarms. It was a step upon the staircase, approaching his room.

He heard it the instant he lay still in bed after the shuffling process known generally as "cuddling down." And he knew that it was approaching because of the assistance the hall clock brought to his bewildered ears. For the hall clock—a big, dignified piece of furniture with a deep note—happened just then to strike the hour of two in the morning, and there was a considerable interval between the two notes. He first heard the step far below in the act of leaving the flagged hall for the staircase; then the clock drowned it with its first stroke, and perhaps a dozen seconds later, when the second stroke had died away, he heard the step again, as it passed from the top of the staircase on to the polished boards of the landing. The owner of the step, meanwhile, had passed up the whole length of the staircase in the interval, and was now coming across the landing in a direct line towards his bedroom door.

"It *is* a step, I suppose," it seems he muttered to himself, as with head partially raised above the blankets he listened intently. "It's a *step*, I mean...?" For the sound was more like a light tapping of a little hammer than an actual step—some hard substance drumming automatically upon the floor, while yet moving in advance. He recognized, however, that there was intelligence behind its movements, because of the sense of direction it displayed, and by the fact that it had turned the sharp corner of the stairs; but the idea presented itself in fugitive fashion to his mind—Heaven alone knows why—that it might be some mechanical contrivance that was worked from the hall by a hand. For the sound was too light to be the tread of a person, yet too "conscious" to be merely a sound of the night operating mechanically. And it was unlike the noise that the feet of any animal would make, any animal that he could think of, that is. A four-footed creature suggested itself to his mind, but without approval.

The puzzling characteristics of the sound, therefore, contradictory as they were, left him utterly perplexed, so that for some little time he could not make up his mind whether to be frightened, interested or merely curious.

This uncertainty, however, lasted but a moment or two at the most, for an appreciable pause outside his door was next followed by a noise of scratching upon the panels, as of hands or paws, and then by the shuffling of some living body that was flattening itself in an attempt to squeeze through the considerable crack between door and flooring, and so to enter the room.

And, hearing it, Spinrobin this time was so petrified with an instantaneous rush of terror, that at first he dared not even move to find the matches again under his pillow.

The pause was dreadful. He longed for brilliant light that should reveal all parts of the room equally, or else for a thick darkness that should conceal him from everything in the world. The uncertain flicker of a single candle playing miserably between the two was the last thing in the world to appeal to him.

And then events crowded too thick and fast for him to recognize any one emotion in particular from all the fire of them passing so swiftly in and out among his hopelessly disorganized thoughts. Terror flashed, but with it flashed also wonder and delight—the audacity of unreflecting courage—and more—even a breathless worship of the powers, knowledge and forces that lifted for him in that little bedroom the vast Transparency that hides from men the Unknown.

It is soon told. For a moment there was silence, and then he knew that the invader had effected an entrance. There was barely time to marvel at the snake-like thinness of the living creature that could avail itself of so narrow a space, when to his amazement he heard the quick patter of feet across the space of boarded flooring next the wall, and then the silence that muffled them as they reached the carpet proper.

Almost at the same second something leaped upon his bed, and there shot swiftly across him a living thing with light, firm tread—a creature, so far as he could form any judgement at all, about the size of a rabbit or a cat. He felt the feet pushing through sheets and blankets upon his body. They were little feet; how many, at that stage, he could not guess. Then he heard the thud as it dropped to the floor upon the other side.

The panic terror that in the dark it would run upon his bare exposed face thus passed; and in that moment of intense relief Spinrobin gripped his soul, so to speak, with both hands and made the effort of his life. Whatever happened now he must have a light, be it only the light of a single miserable candle. In that moment he felt that he would have sacrificed all his hopes of the hereafter to have turned on a flood of searching and brilliant sunshine into every corner of the room—instantaneously. The thought that the creature might jump again upon the bed and touch him before he could see, gave him energy to act.

With dashes of terror shooting through him like spears of ice, he grabbed the matchbox, and after a frenzied entanglement again with sheets and pillowcase, succeeded in breaking four matches in quick succession. They cracked, it seemed to him, like pistol shots, till he half expected that this creature, waiting there in the darkness, must leap out in the direction of the sound to attack him. The fifth lit, and a moment later the candle was burning dimly, but with its usual exasperating leisure and delay. As the flare died down, then gradually rose again, he fairly swallowed the room with a single look, wishing there were eyes all over his body. It was a very faint light. At first he saw nothing, heard nothing—nothing alive, that is.

"I must act! I must do something—at once!" he remembered thinking. For, to wait meant to leave the choice and moment of attack to this other...

Cautiously, and very slowly, therefore, he wriggled to the edge of the bed and slid over, searching with his feet for slippers, but finding none, yet not daring to lower his eyes to look; then stood upright with a sudden rush, shading the candle from his eyes with one hand and peering over it.

As a rule, in moments of overwhelming emotion, the eyes search too eagerly, too furiously, to see properly at all; but this does not seem to have been the case with Spinrobin. The shadows ran about like water and the flickering of the candle-flame dazzled, but there, opposite to him, over by the darkness of the dead fireplace, he saw instantly the small black object that was the immediate cause of his terror. Its actual shape was merged too much in the dark background to be clearly ascertainable, but near the top of it, where presumably the head was, the candle-flame shone reflected in two brilliant points of light that were directed straight upon his face, and he knew that he was looking into the eyes of a living creature that was not the very least on the defensive. It was a living creature, aggressive and unafraid.

For perhaps a couple of minutes—or was it seconds only?—these two beings with the breath of life in them faced one another. Then Spinrobin made a step cautiously in advance; lowering his candle he moved towards it. This he did, partly to see better, partly to protect his bare legs. The idea of protection, however, seems to have been merely instinct, for at once this notion that it might dash forward to attack him was merged in the unaccountable realization of a far grander emotion, as he perceived that this "living creature" facing him was, for all its diminutive size, both dignified and imposing. Something in its atmosphere, something about its mysterious presentment there upon the floor in its dark corner, something, perhaps, that flashed from its brilliant and almost terrible eyes, managed to convey to him that it was clothed with an importance and a significance not attached normally to the animal world. It had "an air." It bore itself with power, with value, almost with pride.

This incongruous impression bereft him of the sensations of ordinary fear, while it increased the sources of his confusion. Yet it convinced. He knew himself face to face with some form of life that was considerable in the true sense—spiritually. It exercised a fascination over him that was at the moment beyond either explanation or belief.

As he moved, moreover, the little dark object also moved—away from him, as though resenting closer inspection. With action—again unlike the action of any animal he could think of, and essentially dignified—both rapid and nicely calculated, it ran towards the curtains behind. This appearance of something stately that went with it was indefinable and beyond everything impressive; for how in the world could such small proportions and diminutive movements convey grandeur? And again Spinrobin found it impossible to decide precisely how it moved—whether on four legs or on two.

Keeping the two points of light always turned upon him, it shot across the floor, leaped easily upon a chair, passed with a nimble spring from this to a table by the wall, still too much in obscurity to permit a proper view; and then, while the amazed secretary approached cautiously to follow its movements better, it crawled to the edge of the table, and in so doing passed for the first time full across the pale zone of flickering candlelight.

Spinrobin, in that quick second, caught a glimpse of flying hair, and saw that it moved either as a human being or as a bird—on two legs.

The same moment it sprang deftly from the high table to the mantelpiece, turned, stood erect, and looked at him with the whole glare of the light upon its face; and Spinrobin, bereft of all power of intelligible sensation whatever, saw to his unutterable distress that it was—a man. The dignity of its movements had already stirred vaguely his sense of awe, but now the realization beyond doubt of its diminutive *human* shape added a singularly acute touch of horror; and it was the combination of the two emotions, possibly, that were responsible also for the two remarkable impulses of which he was first conscious: first, a mad desire to strike and kill; secondly, an imperious feeling that he must hide his eyes in some act or other of worship!

And it was then he realized that the man was—Philip Skale!

Mr. Skale, scarcely a foot high, dressed as usual in black, flowing beard, hooked nose, lambent, flashing eyes and all, stood there upon the mantelpiece level with his secretary's face, not three feet separating them, and—smiled at him. He was small as a Tanagra figure, and in perfect proportion.

It was unspeakably terrible.

II

"Of course—I'm dreaming," cried Spinrobin, half aloud, half to the figure before him. He searched behind him with one hand for solid support. "You're a dream thing. It's some awful trick—God will protect me—!"

Mr. Skale's tiny lips moved. "No, no," his voice said, and it sounded as from a great distance. "I'm no dream thing at all, and you are wide awake. Look at me well. I am the man you know—Philip Skale. Look straight into my eyes and be convinced." Again he smiled his kindly, winning smile. "What you now see is nothing but a result of sounding my true name in a certain way—very softly—to increase the cohesion of my physical molecules and reduce my visible expression. Listen, and watch!"

And Spinrobin, half stupefied, obeyed, feeling that his weakening knees must in another moment give way and precipitate him to the floor. He was utterly unnerved. The onslaught of terror and amazement was overwhelming. For something dreadful beyond all words lay in the sight of this man, whom he was accustomed to reverence in his gigantic everyday shape, here reduced to the stature of a pygmy, yet compelling as ever, terrific even when thus dwarfed. And to hear the voice of thunder that he knew so well come to him disguised within this thin and almost wailing tone, passed equally beyond the limits of what he could feel as emotion or translate into any intelligible words or gesture.

While, therefore, the secretary stood in awful wonder, doing as he was told simply because he could do nothing else, the figure of the clergyman moved with tiny steps to the edge of the mantelpiece, until it seemed as though he meant in another moment to leap on to his companion's shoulder, or into his arms. At the edge, however, he stopped—the brink of a precipice, to him!—and Spinrobin then became aware that from his moving lips, doll-like though bearded, his voice was issuing with an ever-growing volume of sound and power.

Vibrations of swiftly-increasing depth and wavelength were spreading through the air about him, filling the room from floor to ceiling. What the syllables actually uttered may have been he was too dazed to realize, for no degree of concentration was possible to his mind at all; he only knew that, before his smarting eyes, with this rising of the voice to its old dominant inflexion, the figure of Mr. Philip Skale grew likewise, indescribably; swelled, rose, spread upwards and outwards, but with the parts ever passing slowly in consistent inter-relation, from minute to minute. He became, always in perfect proportion, magnified and extended. The growing form, moreover, kept pace exactly, and most beautifully, with the increasing tide of sonorous vibration that flooded himself, its utterer and the whole room.

Spinrobin, it seems, had just sufficient self-control left to realize that this sound was similar in quality to that which had first awakened him and caused the outlines of the furniture to alter, when the sight of Mr. Skale's form changing thus terribly before his eyes, and within the touch of his very hand, became too much for him altogether...

What precisely happened he never knew. The sounds first enveloped him, then drove him backwards with a sense of immense applied resistance. He collapsed upon the sofa a few feet behind him, as though irresistibly pushed. The power that impelled him charged vehemently through the little room till it seemed the walls must burst asunder to give it scope, while the sounds rose to such a volume that he figured himself drowned and overpowered by their mighty vibrations as by the storm swells of the Atlantic. Before he lost them as sound he seems thus to have been aware of them as moving waves of air... The next thing he took in was that amid the waste of silence that now followed his inability to hear, the figure of Philip Skale towered aloft towards the ceiling, till it seemed positively to occupy all the available space in the room about him.

Had he dropped upon the floor instead of upon the sofa it is probable that at this point Spinrobin would have lost consciousness, at any rate for a period; but that sofa, which luckily for his bones was so close behind, galvanized him sharply back into some measure of self-control again. Being provided with powerful springs, it shot him up into the air, whence he relapsed with a series of smaller bounds into a normal sitting posture. Still holding the lighted candle as best he could, the little secretary bounced upon that sofa like a tennis ball. And the violent motion shook him into himself, as it were. His tottering universe struggled back into shape once more. He remembered vaguely that all this was somehow a test of his courage and fitness. And this thought, strengthened by a law of his temperament which forced him to welcome the sweet, mad terror of the whole adventure, helped to call out the reserves of his failing courage.

He bounced upon his feet again—those bare feet plastered with candle grease—and, turning his head, saw the clergyman, of incredible stature, yet still apparently increasing, already over by the door. He was turning the key with a hand the size—O horror!—of Spinrobin's breast. The next moment his vast stooping body filled the entire entrance, blotting out whole portions of the walls on either side, then was gone from the room.

Leaving the candlestick on the sofa, his heart aflame with a fearful ecstasy of curiosity, he dashed across the floor in pursuit, but Mr. Skale, silently and with the swiftness of a river, was already down the stairs before he had covered half the distance.

Through the framework of the door Spinrobin saw this picture:

Skale, like some awful Cyclops, stood upon the floor of the hall some twenty feet below, yet rearing terrifically up through the well of the building till his head and shoulders alone seemed to fill the entire space beneath the skylight. Though his feet rested unquestionably upon the ground, his face, huge as a planet in the sky, rose looming and half lighted above the banisters of this second storey, his tangled locks sweeping the ceiling, and his beard, like some dark river of hair, flowing downwards through the night. And this spreading countenance of cloud it was, hanging in the semi-darkness, that Spinrobin saw turn slowly towards him across the faint flicker of the candlelight, look straight down into his face, and smile. The great mouth and eyes unquestionably smiled. And that smile, for all its vast terror, was beyond words enchanting—like the spread laughter of a summer landscape.

Among the spaces of the immense visage—reminding him curiously of his boyhood's conception of the Creator—Spinrobin lost himself and grew dizzy with a deadly yet delicious faintness. The mighty tenderness, the compassion, the splendour of that giant smile overpowered him and swallowed him up.

For one second, in dreadful silence, he gazed. Then, rising to meet the test with a courage that he felt might somehow involve the alteration if not the actual destruction of his own little personality, but that also proved his supreme gameness at the same time, he tried to smile in return... The strange and pitiful attempt upon his own face perhaps, in the semi-obscurity, was not seen. He only remembers that he somehow found strength to crawl forward and close the door with a bang, though not the strength to turn the key and lock it, and that two seconds later, having kicked the candle over and out in his flying leap, he was in the middle of the bed under a confused pile of sheets and blankets, weeping with muffled sobs in the darkness as though his heart must burst with the wonder and terror of all he had witnessed.

For, to the simple in heart, at the end of all possible stress and strain of emotion, comes mercifully the blinding relief of tears...

And then, although too overcome to be able to prove it even to himself, it was significant that, lying there smothered among the bedclothes, he became aware of the presence of something astonishingly sweet and comforting in his consciousness. It came quite suddenly upon him; the reaction he experienced, he says, was very wonderful, for with it the sense of absolute safety and security returned to him. Like a terrified child in the darkness who suddenly knows that its mother stands by the bed, all-powerful to soothe, he felt certain that some one had moved into the room, was close beside him, and was even trying to smooth his pillow and arrange the twisted bedclothes.

He did not dare uncover his face to see, for he was still dominated by the memory of Mr. Skale's portentous visage; but his ears were not so easily denied, and he was positive that he heard a voice that called his name as though it were the opening phrase of some sweet, childhood lullaby. There was a touch about him somewhere, it seemed, of delicate cool hands that brought with them the fragrance as of a scented summer wind; and the last thing he remembered before he sank away into welcome unconsciousness was an impression, fugitive and dreamlike, of a gentle face, unstained and pale as marble, that bent above his pillow, and, singing, called him away to forgetfulness and peace.

III

And several hours later, when he woke after a refreshing sleep to find Mrs. Mawle smiling down upon him over a tray of steaming coffee, he recalled the events of the night with a sense of vivid reality that if possible increased his conviction of their truth, but without the smallest symptom of terror or dismay. For the blessing of the presence that had soothed him into sleep lay still upon him like a garment to protect. The test had come and he had not wholly failed.

With something approaching amusement, he watched the housekeeper pick up a candlestick from the middle of the floor and put his Jaeger slippers beneath the chair, having found one by the cupboard and the other over by the fireplace.

"Mr. Skale's compliments and Mr. Spinrobin is not to hurry himself," he heard her saying, as she put the tray beside the bed and went out of the room. He looked at his watch and saw that it was after ten o'clock.

Half an hour later he was dressed and on his way downstairs, conscious only of an overwhelming desire to see Mr. Skale, but to see him in his normal and fatherly aspect again. For a strain of worship mingled oddly with his devouring curiosity, and he was thirsty now for the rest of the adventure, for the complete revelation of the Discovery in all its bearings. And the moment he saw the clergyman in the hall he ran towards him, scarcely realizing what it was he meant to say or do. Mr. Skale stretched out both hands to meet him. His face was alight with pleasure.

But, before they could meet and touch, a door opened and in slipped Miriam between them; she, too, was radiant, and her hands outstretched.

"Me first, please! Me first!" she cried with happy laughter, and before Spinrobin realized what was happening, she had flung her arms about his neck and kissed him. "You were splendid!" she whispered in his ear, "and I *am* proud of you—ever so proud!"

The next minute Skale had him by the hands.

"Well done! well done!" his voice boomed, while he gazed down into his face with enthusiastic and unqualified approval. "It was all magnificent. My dear little fellow, you've got the heart of a god, and, by Heavens, you shall become as a god too! For you are worthy!" He shook him violently by both hands, while Miriam looked eagerly on with admiration in her wide grey eyes.

"I'm so glad, so awfully glad—" stammered the secretary, remembering with shame his moments of vivid terror. He hardly knew what he said at the moment.

"The properties of things," thundered the clergyman, "as you have now learned, are merely the 'muffled utterances of the Sounds that made them.' The thing itself is its name."

He spoke rapidly, with intense ardour and with reverence. "You have seen with your own eyes a scientific proof of my Discovery on its humblest level—how the physical properties of objects can be manipulated by the vibratory utterance of their true names—can be extended, reduced, glorified. Next you shall learn that spiritual qualities—the attributes of higher states of being—can be similarly dealt with and harnessed—exalted, intensified, *invoked*—and that the correct utterance of mighty Names can seduce their specific qualities into your own soul to make you mighty and eternal as themselves, and that to call upon the Great Names is no idle phrase... When the time comes, Spinrobin, you shall not shrink, you shall not shrink..." He flung his arms out with a great gesture of delight.

"No," repeated Spinrobin, yet aware that he felt mentally battered at the prospect, "I shall not shrink. I think—now—I can manage—anything!"

And then, watching Miriam with lingering glance as she vanished laughing up the staircase, he followed Mr. Skale into the library, his thoughts tearing wildly to and fro, swelling with delight and pride, thrilling with the wonder of what was yet to come. There, with fewest possible sentences, the clergyman announced that he now accepted him and would, therefore, carry out the promise with regard to the bequeathal of his property to him in the event of any untoward circumstances arising later. He also handed to him in cash the salary for the "trial month," together with a cheque for the first quarter in advance. He was beaming with the satisfaction he felt at having found at last a really qualified helper. Spinrobin looked into his face as they shook hands over the bargain. He was thinking of other aspects he had seen of this amazing being but a few hours before—the minute, the colossal, the changing-between-the-two Skales...

"I'm game, Mr. Skale," he said simply, forgetting all his recent doubts and terrors.

"I know you are," the clergyman replied. "I knew it all along."

I

The first thing Spinrobin knew when he ran upstairs to lock away the money in his desk was that his whole being, without his directing it, asked a question of momentous import. He did not himself ask it deliberately. He surprised his sub-consciousness asking it:

"WHAT IS THIS NAME THAT PHILIP SKALE FOR EVER SEEKS?"

It was no longer mere curiosity that asked it, but that sense of responsibility which in all men of principle and character lies at the root of action and of life. And Spinrobin, for all his little weaknesses, was a man of character and principle. There came a point when he could no longer follow blindly where others led, even though the leader were so grand an individual as Philip Skale. This point is reached at varying degrees of the moral thermometer, and but for the love that Miriam had wakened in his heart, it might have taken much longer to send the mercury of his will so high in so short a time. He now felt responsibility for two, and in the depths of his queer, confused, little mind stirred the thought that possibly after all the great adventure he sought was only the supreme adventure of a very wonderful Love.

He records these two questions at this point, and it is only just to himself, therefore, to set them down here. To neither was the answer yet forthcoming.

For some days the routine of this singular household followed its normal course, the only change being that while the secretary practised his Hebrew names and studied the relations between sound, colour, form and the rest, he kept himself a little better in hand, for Love is a mighty humanizer and holds down the nose upon the grindstone of the wholesome and practical values of existence. He turned, so to speak, and tried to face the matter squarely; to see the adventure as a whole; to get all round it and judge. It seems, however, that he was too much in the thick of it to get that bird's-eye view which reduces details to the right proportion. Skale's personality was too close, and flooded him too violently. Spinrobin remained confused and bewildered; but also unbelievably happy.

"Coming out all right," he wrote shakily in that gilt-edged diary. "Beginning to understand why I'm in the world. Am just as important as anybody else—*really*. Impossible explain more." His entries were very like telegrams, in which a man attempts to express in a lucid shorthand all manner of things that the actual words hardly compass. And life itself is not unlike some mighty telegram that seeks vainly to express, between the extremes of silence and excess, all that the soul would say...

"Skale is going too far," perhaps best expresses the daily burden of his accumulating apprehension. "He is leading up to something that makes me shrink—something not quite legitimate. Playing with an Olympian fire that may consume us both." And there his telegram stopped; for how in the world could he put into mere language the pain and distress involved in the thought that it might at the same time consume Miriam? It all touched appalling depths of awe in his soul. It made his heart shake. The girl had become a part of his very self.

Vivid reactions he suffered, alternating with equally vivid enthusiasms. He realized how visionary the clergyman's poetical talk was, but the next minute the practical results staggered him again, as it were, back into a state of conviction. For the poetry obscured his judgement and fired his imagination so that he could not follow calmly. The feeling that it was not only illogical but insane troubled him; yet the physical effects stared him in the face, and to argue with physical results is waste of time. One must act.

Yet how "act?" The only way that offered he accepted: he fell back upon the habits of his boyhood, read his Bible, and at night dropped humbly upon his knees and prayed.

"Keep me straight and pure and simple, and bless... Miriam. Grant that I may love and strengthen her... and that my love may bring her peace... and joy... and guide me through all this terror, I beseech Thee, into Truth..."

For, in the beauty of his selfless love, he dared not even admit that it was love; feeling only the highest, he could not quite correlate his sweet and elevated passion with the common standards of what the World called love. The humility of a great love is ever amazing.

And then followed in his prayers the more cowardly cry for ordinary protection from the possible results of Skale's audacity. The Love of God he could understand, but the Wrath of God was a conception he was still unemancipated enough to dread; and a dark, portentous terror that Skale might incur it, and that he might be dragged at its heels into some hideous catastrophe, chased him through the days and nights. It all seemed so unlawful, impious, blasphemous...

"... And preserve us from vain presumptions of the heart and brain, I pray Thee, lest we be consumed... Please, O God, forgive the insolence of our wills... and the ignorant daring of our spirit... Permit not the innocent to suffer for the guilty... and especially bless... Miriam..."

Yet through it all ran that exquisite memory of the calling of his true name in the spaces of his soul. The beauty of far-off unattainable things hovered like a star above his head, so that he went about the house with an insatiable yearning in his heart, a perpetual smile of wonder upon his face, and in his eyes a gleam that was sometimes terror, sometimes delight.

It was almost as if some great voice called to him from the mountaintops, and the little chap was forever answering in his heart, "I'm coming! I'm coming!" and then losing his way purposely, or hiding behind bushes on the way for fear of meeting the great invisible Caller face to face.

II

And, meanwhile, the house became for him a kind of Sound-Temple as it were, protected from desecration by the hills and desolate spaces that surrounded it. From dawn to darkness its halls and corridors echoed with the singing violin, Skale's booming voice, Miriam's gentle tones, and his own plaintive yet excited note, while outside the old grey walls the air was ever alive with the sighing of the winds and the ceaseless murmur of falling water. Even at night the place was not silent. He understood at last what the clergyman had told him—that perfect silence does not exist. The universe, down to its smallest detail, sings through every second of time.

The sounds of nature especially haunted him. He never heard the wind now without thinking of lost whispers from the voice of God that had strayed down upon the world to sweeten and bewilder the hearts of men—whispers a-search for listeners simple enough to understand. And when their walks took them as far as the sea, the dirge of the waves troubled his soul with a kind of distressing exaltation that afflicted the very deeps of his being. It was with a new comprehension he understood his employer's dictum that the keynote of external nature was middle F—this employer who himself possessed that psychic sense of absolute pitch—and that the roar of a city, wind in forest trees, the cry of trains, the rushing of rivers and falling water, Niagara itself, all produced this single utterance; and he loved to sing it on the moors, Miriam laughing by his side, and to realize that the world, literally, sang with them.

Behind all sounds he divined for the first time a majesty that appalled; his imagination, glorified by Skale, instantly fell to constructing the forms they bodied forth. Out of doors the flutes of Pan cried to him to dance: indoors the echoes of yet greater music whispered in the penetralia of his spirit that he should cry. In this extraordinary new world of Philip Skale's revelation he fairly spun.

It was one thing when the protective presence of the clergyman was about him, or when he was sustained by the excitement of enthusiasm, but when he was alone, at his normal level, timid, yet adventurous, the too vivid sense of these new things made him tremble. The terrifying beauty of Skale's ideas; the realization in cold blood that all forms in the world about him were silently a-singing, and might any moment vanish and release their huge bodies into primal sounds; that the stones in the road, the peaked hills, the very earth herself might alter in shape before his eyes: on the other hand, that the viewless forces of life and death might leap into visibility and form with the calling of their names; that himself, and Skale, and Mrs. Mawle, and that pale fairy girl-figure were all enmeshed in the same scheme with plants, insects, animals and planets; and that God's voice was everywhere too sublimely close—all this, when he was alone, oppressed him with a sense of things that were too intimate and too mighty for daily life.

In these moments—so frequent now as to be almost continuous—he preferred the safety of his ordinary and normal existence, dull though it might be; the limited personality he had been so anxious to escape from seemed wondrous sweet and comforting.

The Terror of the approaching Experiment with this mighty name appalled him.

The forces, thus battling within his soul, became more and more contradictory and confused. The outcome for himself seemed to be the result of the least little pressure this way or that—possibly at the very last moment, too. Which way the waiting Climax might draw him was a question impossible to decide.

III

And then, suddenly, the whole portentous business moved a sharp stage nearer that hidden climax, when one afternoon Mr. Skale came up unexpectedly behind him and laid a great hand upon his shoulder in a way that made him positively jump.

"Spinrobin," he said, in those masterful, resonant tones that shamed his timidity and cowardice, "are you ready?"

"For anything and everything," was the immediate reply, given almost automatically as he felt the clergyman's forces flood into his soul and lift him.

"The time is at hand, then," continued the other, leading his companion by the arm to a deep leather sofa, "for you to know certain things that for your own safety and ours, I was obliged to keep hidden till now—first among which is the fact that this house is not, as you supposed, empty."

Prepared as he was for some surprising announcement, Spinrobin nevertheless started. It was so abrupt.

"Not empty!" he repeated, eager to hear more, yet quaking. He had never forgotten the nightly sounds and steps in his own passage.

"The rooms beyond your own," said Skale, with a solemnity that amounted to reverence, "are occupied—"

"By—" gasped the secretary.

"Captured Sounds—gigantic," was the reply, uttered almost below the breath.

The two men looked steadily at one another for the space of several seconds, Spinrobin charged to the brim with anxious questions pressing somehow upon the fringe of life and death, Skale obviously calculating how much he might reveal or how little.

"Mr. Spinrobin," he said presently, holding him firmly with his eyes, "you are aware by this time that what I seek is the correct pronunciation of certain names—of a certain name, let us say, and that so complex is the nature of this name that no single voice can utter it. I need a chord, a human chord of four voices."

Spinrobin bowed.

"After years of research and experiment," resumed the clergyman, "I have found the first three notes, and now, in your own person, has come my supreme happiness in the discovery of the fourth. What I now wish you to know, though I cannot expect you to understand it all at first, is that the name I seek is broken up into four great divisions of sound, and that to each of these separate divisions the four notes of our chord form introductory channels. When the time comes to utter it, each one of us will call the syllable or sound that awakens the mighty response in one of these immense and terrific divisions, so that the whole name will vibrate as a single chord sung perfectly in tune."

Mr. Skale paused and drew deep breaths. This approach to his great experiment, even in speech, seemed to exhaust him so that he was obliged to call upon reserves of force that lay beneath. His whole manner betrayed the gravity, the reverence, the mingled respect and excitement of—death.

And the simple truth is that at the moment Spinrobin could not find in himself sufficient courage to ask what this fearful and prodigious name might be. Even to put ordinary questions about the four rooms was a little beyond him, for his heart beat like a hammer against his ribs, and he heard its ominous drum sounding through both his temples.

"And in each of the rooms in your corridor, ready to leap forth when called, lie the sounds or voices I have captured and imprisoned, these separate chambers being sheeted and prepared—huge wax receptacles, in fact, akin to the cylinders of the phonograph. Together with the form or pattern belonging to them, and the colour, there they lie at present in silence and invisibility, just as the universe lay in silence and invisibility before the word of God called it into objective being. But—*know them and they are mine.*"

"All these weeks—so close to me," whispered Spinrobin, too low for Skale to notice.

Then the clergyman leaned over towards him. "These captured sounds are as yet by no means complete," he said through his beard, as though afraid to admit it; "for all I have of them really is their initial letters, of their forms the merest faint outlines, and of their colours but a first suggestion. And we must be careful, we must be absolutely wise. To utter them correctly will mean to transfer to us the qualities of Gods, whereas to utter falsely may mean to release upon the surface of the world forces that—" He shrugged his great shoulders and an ashen pallor spread downwards over the face to the very lips. The sentence remained unfinished; and its very incompleteness left Spinrobin with the most grievous agony of apprehension he had yet experienced.

"So that, if you are ready, our next step shall be to show you the room in which your own particular sound lies," added Mr. Skale after a long pause; "the sound in the chord it will be your privilege to utter when the time comes. For each of us will utter his or her particular letter, the four together making up the first syllable in the name I seek."

Mr. Skale looked steadily down into the wide blue eyes of his companion, and for some minutes neither of them spoke.

"The letter I am to utter," repeated the secretary at length; "the letter in some great name?"

Mr. Skale smiled upon him with the mighty triumph of the Promethean idea in his eyes.

"The room," he muttered deeply and softly, "in which it lies waiting for you to claim it at the appointed time... the room where you shall learn its colour, become attuned to its great vibratory activity, see its form, and *know* its power in your own person."

Again they looked long into one another's eyes.

"I'm game," murmured Spinrobin almost inaudibly; "I'm game, Mr. Skale." But, as he said it, something in his round head turned dizzy, while his thoughts flew to Miriam and to the clergyman's significant phrase of a few minutes ago—"we must be careful, we must be absolutely wise."

IV

And the preparation the clergyman insisted upon—detailed, thorough and scrupulous—certainly did not lessen in Spinrobin's eyes the gravity of the approaching ordeal. They spent two days and nights in the very precise and punctilious study, and utterance, of the Hebrew names of the "angels"—that is, forces—whose qualities were essential to their safety.

Also, at the same time, they fasted.

But when the time came for the formal visit to those closed rooms, of which the locked doors were like veils in a temple, Spinrobin declares it made him think of some solemn procession down ancient passageways of crypt or pyramid to the hidden places where inscrutable secrets lay. It was certainly thrilling and impressive. Skale went first, moving slowly with big strides, grave as death, and so profoundly convinced of the momentous nature of their errand that an air of dignity, and of dark adventure almost majestic, hung about his figure. The long corridor, that dreary December morning, stretched into a world of shadows, and about halfway down it he halted in front of a door next but one to Spinrobin's room and turned towards his companion.

Spinrobin, in a mood to see anything, yet striving to hide behind one of those "bushes," as it were, kept his distance a little, but Mr. Skale took him by the arm and drew him forward to his side. Slowly he stooped, till the great bearded lips were level with his ear, and whispered solemnly:

"Blessed are the pure in heart, for they shall see—and *hear* God."

Then he turned the key and led the way inside.

But apparently there were double doors, for they found themselves at first in a cupboard-like space that formed a tiny vestibule to the room itself; and here there was light enough to see that the clergyman was taking from nails on the wall two long garments like surplices, coloured, so far as Spinrobin could make out, a deep red and a deep violet.

"For our protection," whispered Skale, enveloping himself in the red one, while he handed the other to his companion and helped him into it. "Wear it closely about your body until we come out." And while the secretary struggled among the folds of this cassock-like garment, that was several feet too long for his diminutive stature, the clergyman added, still with a gravity and earnestness that impressed the imagination beyond all reach of the ludicrous:

"For sound and colour are intimately associated, and there are combinations of the two that can throw the spiritual body into a condition of safe receptivity, without which we should be deaf and blind even in the great Presences themselves."

Trivial details, presenting themselves in really dramatic moments, may impress the mind with extraordinary aptness. At this very moment Spinrobin's eyes noticed in the corner of wall and door a tiny spider's web, with the spider itself hanging in the centre of its little net—shaking. And he has never forgotten it. It expressed pictorially exactly what he felt himself. He, too, felt that he was shaking in midair—as in the centre of a web whose strands hung suspended from the very stars.

And the words, spoken in that slow deep whisper, filled the little space in which the two men stood, and somehow completed for Spinrobin the sense of stupendous things adequately approached.

Then Mr. Skale closed the outer door, shutting out the last feeble glimmer of day, at the same moment turning the handle of the portal beyond. And as they entered the darkness, Spinrobin, holding up his violet robe with one hand to prevent tripping, with the other caught hold of the tail of the flowing garment in front of him. For a second or two he stopped breathing altogether.

v

On the very threshold a soft murmur of beauty met them; and, as plainly as though the darkness had lifted into a blaze of light, the secretary at once realized that he stood in the presence of something greater than all he had hitherto known in this world. He had managed to find the clergyman's big hand, and he held it tightly through a twisted corner of his voluminous robe. The inner door next closed behind them. Skale, he was aware, had again stooped in the darkness to the level of his ear.

"I'll give you the sound—the note," he heard him whisper. "Utter it inwardly—in your thoughts only. Its vibrations correspond to the colour, and will protect us."

"Protect us?" gasped Spinrobin with dry lips.

"From being shattered and destroyed—owing to the intense activity of the vibrations conveyed to our ultimate physical atoms," was the whispered reply, as the clergyman proceeded to give him under his breath a one-syllable sound that was unlike any word he knew, and that for the life of him he has never been able to reproduce since.

Mr. Skale straightened himself up again and Spinrobin pictured him standing there twice his natural size, a huge and impressive figure as he had once before seen him, clothed now with the double dignity of his strange knowledge. Then, advancing slowly to the centre of the room, they stood still, each uttering silently in his thoughts the syllable that attuned their inner beings to safety.

Almost immediately, as the seconds passed, the secretary became aware that the room was beginning to shake with a powerful but regular movement. All about him had become alive. Vitality, like the vitality of youth upon mountain tops, pulsed and whirled about them, pouring into them the currents of a rushing glorious life, undiluted, straight from the source. In his little person he felt both the keenness of sharp steel and the vast momentum of a whole ocean. Thus he describes it. And the more clearly he uttered in his thoughts the sound given to him by his leader, the greater seemed the influx of strength and glory into his heart.

The darkness, meanwhile, began to lift. It moved upwards in spirals that, as they rose, hummed and sang. A soft blaze of violet like the colour of the robe he wore became faintly visible in the air. The chamber, he perceived, was about the same size as his own bedroom, and empty of all furniture, while walls, floor, and ceiling were draped in the same shade of violet that covered his shoulders; and the sound he uttered, *and thought*, called forth the colour and made it swim into visibility. The walls and ceiling sheeted with wax opened, so to speak, their giant lips.

Mr. Skale made a movement and drew him closer. He raised one arm into the air, and Spinrobin, following the motion, saw what at first he imagined to be vast round faces glimmering overhead, outlined darkly against the violet atmosphere. Mr. Skale, with what seemed a horrible audacity, was reaching up to touch them, and as he did so there issued a low, soft, metallic sound, humming and melodious, that dropped sweetly about his ears. Then the secretary saw that they were discs of metal—immense gongs swinging in midair, suspended in some way from the ceiling, and each one as Skale touched it emitted its beautiful note till all combined together at length into a single chord.

And this chord, though Spinrobin talks whole pages in describing it, apparently brought in its train the swell and thunder of something beyond,—the far sweetness of exquisite harmonics, thousands upon thousands, inwoven with the strands of deeper notes that boomed with colossal vibrations about them. And, in some fashion that musical people will understand, its gentler notes caught up the sound that Spinrobin was uttering in his mind, and took possession of it. They merged. An extraordinary volume, suggesting a huge aggregation of sound behind it—in the same way that a murmur of wind may suggest the roar of tempests—rose and fell through the room, lifted them up, bore them away, sang majestically over their heads, under their feet, and through their very minds. The vibrations of their own physical atoms fell into pace with these other spiritual activities by a kind of sympathetic resonance.

The combination of power and simplicity was what impressed him most, it seems, for it resembled—resembled only—the great spiritual simplicity in Beethoven that rouses and at the same time satisfies the profoundest yearnings of the soul. It swept him into utter bliss, into something for once complete. And Spinrobin, at the centre of his glorified yet quaking little heart, understood vaguely that the sound he uttered, and the sound he heard, were directly connected with the presence of some august and awful Name...

VI

Suddenly Mr. Skale, he was aware, became rigid beside him. Spinrobin pressed closer, seeking the protective warmth of his body, and realizing from the gesture that something new was about to happen. And something did happen, though not precisely in the sense that things happen in the streets and in the markets of men. In the sphere of his mind, perhaps, it happened, but was none the less real for that.

For the Presence he had been aware of in the room from the moment of entrance became then suddenly almost concrete. It came closer—sheeted in wonder inscrutable. The form and body of the sounds that filled the air pressed forward into partial visibility. Spinrobin's powers of interior sight, he dimly realized, increased at the same time. Vast as a mountain, as a whole range of mountains; beautiful as a star, as a whole heaven of stars; yet simple as a flower of the field; and singing this little song of pure glory and joy that he felt was the inmost message of the chord—this Presence in the room sought to push forward into objective reality. And behind it, he knew, lay the stupendous urgency and drive of some power that held the entire universe in its pulses as easily as the ocean holds a shoal of minnows...

But the limits of realization for him were almost reached. Spinrobin wanted to close his eyes, yet could not. He was driven along with the wave of sound thus awakened and forced to see what was to be seen. This time there was no bush behind which he could screen himself. And there, dimly sketched out of the rhythmical vibrations of the seething violet obscurity, rose that looming Outline of wonder and majesty that clothed itself about them with a garment as of visible sound. The Unknown, suggesting incredible dimensions, stood at his elbow, tremendously draped in these dim, voluminous folds of music and colour—very fearful, very seductive, yet so supremely simple at the same time that a little child could have understood without fear.

But only partially there, only partially revealed. The ineffable glory was never quite told. Spinrobin, amid all the torrent of words in which he sought later to describe the experience, could only falter out a single comprehensible sentence: "I felt like stammering in intoxication over the first letter of a name I loved—loved to the point of ecstasy—to the point even of giving up my life for it."

And meanwhile, breathless and shaking, he clung to Skale, still murmuring in his heart the magic syllable, but swept into some region of glory where pain and joy both ceased, where terror and delight merged into some perfectly simple form of love, and where he became in an instant of time an entirely new and emancipated Spinrobin, driving at full speed towards the ultimate sound and secret of the universe—God.

He never remembered exactly how he got out of the room, but it always seemed as though he dropped with a crash from some enormous height. The sounds ceased; the gongs died into silence; the violet faded; the quivering wax lay still... Mr. Skale was moving beside him, and the next minute they were in the narrow vestibule between the doors, hanging up ordinary coloured surplices upon ordinary iron nails.

Spinrobin stumbled. Skale caught him. They were in the corridor again—cold, cheerless, full of December murk and shadows—and the secretary was leaning against the clergyman's shoulder breathless and trembling as though he had run a mile.

I

"And the colour of *my* sound is a pale green," he heard behind him in tones as sweet as a muted violin string, "while the form of my note fits into yours just like a glove. Dear Spinny, don't tremble so. We shall always be together, remember, you and I..."

And when, turning, he saw Miriam at his side, radiant with her shining little smile of welcome, the relief was so great that he took her in his arms and would not let her go. She drew him tenderly away downstairs, for the clergyman, it seemed, was still busy with something in the room, and had left them...

"*I* know, *I* know," she said softly, making him sit down beside her on the sofa, "I know the rush of pain and happiness it brings. It shifts the whole key of your life, doesn't it? When I first went into my 'room' and learned the letter I was to utter in the Name, I felt as if I could never come back to ordinary things again, or—"

"What name?" interrupted Spinrobin, drawing sharply away from her, and the same second amazed at the recklessness that had prompted the one question he dreaded.

The inevitable reaction had come. He realized for the first time that there *was* an alternative. All the passion of battle was upon him. The terrific splendours of Skale's possible achievement dazzled the very windows of his soul, but at the same time the sweet uses of normal human life called searchingly to him from within. He had been circling about this fight for days; at last it was unexpectedly upon him. He might climb to Skale's impossible Heaven, Skale's outrageous Heaven... on the wings of this portentous experience, or—he might sink back into the stream of wholesome and commonplace life, with a delicious little human love to companion him across the years, the unsoiled love of an embryonic soul that he could train practically from birth. Miriam was beside him, soft and yielding, ready, doubtless, to be moulded for either path.

"What name?" he repeated, holding his breath once the words were out.

"*The* name, of course," she answered gently, smiling up into his eyes. "The name I have lived to know and that you came here to learn, so that when our voices sing and utter it together in the chord we shall both become—"

Spinrobin set his mouth against her own to stop her speech. She yielded to him with her whole little body. Her eyes smiled the great human welcome as she stared so closely into his.

"Shall become—what we are not now," he cried fiercely, drawing his face back, but holding her body yet more closely to him. "Lose each other, don't you see? Don't you realize that?"

"No, no," she said faintly, "find each other—you mean—"

"Yes—if all goes well!" He spoke the words very low. For perhaps thirty seconds they stared most searchingly into each other's eyes, drawing slightly apart. Very slowly her face, then, went exceedingly pale.

"*If—all goes well*," she repeated, horrified. Then, after a pause, she added: "You mean—that he might make a mistake—or—?"

And Spinrobin, drinking in the sweet breath that bore the words so softly from her lips, answered, measuring his words with ponderous gravity as though each conveyed a sentence of life or death, "*If—all—goes—well.*"

She watched him with something of that utter clinging mother-love in her eyes that claims any degree of suffering gladly rather than the loss of her own—passionately welcoming misery in preference to loss. She, too, had divined the alternative.

Then, kissing his cheeks and eyes and lips, she untied his arms from about her neck and ran, blushing furiously, from the room. And with her went doubt, for the first time—doubt as to the success of the great experiment—doubt as to their Leader's power.

II

And while Spinrobin still sat there, trembling with the two passions that tore his soul in twain—the passion to climb forbidden skies with Skale, and the passion to know sweet human love with Miriam—there came thundering into the room no less a personage than the giant clergyman, straight from those haunted rooms. Pallor hung about his face, but there was a light radiating through it—a high, luminous whiteness—that made the secretary think of his childhood's pictures of the Hebrew prophet descending from Mount Sinai, the glory of internal spheres still reflected upon the skin and eyes. Skale, like a flame and a wind, came pouring into the room. The thing he had remained upstairs to complete had clearly proved successful. The experiment had moved another stage—almost the final one—nearer accomplishment.

The reaction was genuinely terrific. Spinrobin felt himself swept away beyond all power of redemption. Miriam and the delicious human life faded into insignificance again. What, in the name of the eternal fires, were a girl's lips and love compared to the possibilities of Olympian achievement promised by Skale's golden audacities? Earth faded before the lights of heaven. The whole tide of human emotion was nothing compared to a drop of this terrible salt brine from seas in unknown stars... As usual Skale's personality caught him up into some seventh heaven of the soaring imagination.

"Spinrobin, my glorious companion in adventure," thundered the clergyman, "your note suits perfectly the chord! I am delighted beyond all words. You chime with amazing precision and accuracy into the complex Master-Tone I need for the proper pronunciation of the Name! Your coming has been an inspiration permitted of Him who owns it." His excitement was profoundly moving. The man was in earnest if ever man was. "We shall succeed!" And he caught him in his arms. "For the Name manifests the essential attributes of the Being it describes, and in uttering it we shall know mystical union with it... We shall be as Gods!"

"Splendid! Splendid!" exclaimed Spinrobin, utterly carried away by this spiritual enthusiasm. "I will follow you to the end—"

III

The words were scarcely out of his mouth when framed in the doorway, delicate and seductive as a witch, again stood Miriam, then moved softly forward into the room. Her face was pale as the grave. Her little, delicate mouth was set with resolution. Clearly she had overheard, but clearly also she had used the interval for serious reflection.

"We cannot possibly—*fail*, can we?" she asked, gliding up like a frightened fawn to the clergyman's side.

He turned upon her, stern, even terrible. So relentless was his swift appearance, so implacable in purpose, that Spinrobin felt the sudden impulse to fly to her assistance. But instantly his great visage broke into a smile like the smile of thunderous clouds when unexpectedly the sun breaks through, then quickly hides itself again.

"Everywhere," he roared, "true things are great and clean... Have faith... have faith..." And he looked upon them both as though his eyes would sweep from their petty souls all vestige of what was afraid and immature. "We all are—pure... we all are true... each calls his note in singleness of heart... we cannot fail!"

And just here Spinrobin, a little beyond himself with excitement probably, pattered across the room to his giant leader's side and peered up into his visage. He stood on tiptoe, craning his neck forwards, then spoke very low:

"I have the right, *we* have the right—for I have earned it—to be taken now fully into confidence, and to know everything—*everything*," came the words; and the reply, simple and immediate, that dropped back upon him through all that tangle of ragged beard was brief and to the point:

"You have. Listen, then—" And he led them both by the hand like two children towards the sofa, and then, standing over them, began to speak.

IV

"I seek," he said slowly and gravely, "the correct utterance of a certain mighty and ineffable name, and in each of those four rooms lies a letter of its first syllable. For all these years of research"—his voice dropped suddenly—"have only brought me to that—the first syllable. And the name itself is composed of four, each more mighty than the last."

A violent trembling ran over both listeners. Spinrobin, holding a cold little hand in his, dreaded unuttered sentences. For if mere letters could spell so vast a message, what must be the meaning of a whole syllable, and what the dire content of the completed name itself!

"Yes," Skale went on with a reverence born of profoundest awe, "the captured sounds I hold are but the opening vibrations of this tremendous name, and the task is of such magnitude that absolute courage and absolute faith are essential. For the sounds are themselves creative sounds, and the consequences in case of faulty utterance might be too appalling to contemplate—"

"Creative!" fell from the little man on the sofa, aghast at the possibility. Yet the one burning question that lay trembling just behind his lips dared not frame itself in words, for there was something in Mr. Skale's face and manner that rendered the asking of it not yet possible. The revelation of the name must wait.

"Even singly, as you saw, their power is terrific," he went on, ignoring the pathetic interruption, "but united—as we shall unite them while each of us utters his letter and summons forth the entire syllable by means of the chord—they will constitute a Word of Power which shall make us as Gods if uttered correctly; if incorrectly, shall pour from this house to consume and alter the surface of the entire world with the destructive tempest due to mispronunciation and a lie."

Miriam nestled closer into her companion's side. There was otherwise no sign outwardly of the emotions that surged through the two little figures upon the sofa.

"And now—now that you have this first syllable complete?" faltered a high and sharing tenor voice.

"We must transfer it to a home where it shall wait in silence and in safety until we have also captured the other remaining three." Skale came forward and lowered his mouth to his companions' ears. "We shall transfer it, as you now understand, by chanting the four letters. Our living chord will summon forth that first syllable into visible form and shape. Our four voices, thus trained and purified, each singing a mighty letter, shall create the astounding pattern of the name's first syllable—"

"But the home," stammered Spinrobin; "this home where it shall await the rest?"

"My rooms," was the reply, "can contain letters only, for a whole syllable I need a larger space. In the crypt-like cellars beneath this house I have the necessary space all ready and prepared to hold this first syllable while we work upon the second. Come, and you shall see!"

They crossed the hall and went down the long stone passage beyond the dining room till they reached a swinging baize door, and so came to the dark stairs that plunged below ground. Skale strode first, Spinrobin following with beating heart; he held Miriam by the hand; his steps, though firm enough, made him think of his efforts as a boy when treading water for solid ground out of his depth.

V

Cold air met them, yet it was neither dank nor unpleasant as air usually is that has never tasted sunlight. There was a touch of vitality about it wholly remarkable. Miriam pressed closer. Every detail, every little incident that brought them nearer to the climax was now interpreted by these two loving children as something that might eventually spell for them separation. Yet neither referred to it directly. The pain of the ultimate choice possessed them deep within.

"Here," exclaimed the clergyman in a hushed tone that yet woke echoes on all sides, while he lit a candle and held it aloft, "you see the cellar vaults all ready for the first great syllable when our chord shall bring it leaping down from the rooms upstairs. Here will reside the pattern of the name's opening syllable till we shall have accomplished the construction of the others."

And like some august master of forbidden ceremonies, looking twice his natural size as the shadows played tricks with his arms and shoulders, merging his outline into walls and ceiling, Skale stood and looked about him.

Spaces stretched away on all sides as in the crypt of a cathedral, most beautifully and harmoniously draped with the separate colours of the four rooms, red, yellow, violet and green; immense gongs, connected apparently with some intricate network of shining wires, hung suspended in midair beneath the arches; rising from the floor were gigantic tuning forks, erect and silent, immediately behind which gaped artificial air-cavities placed to increase the intensity of the respective notes when caught; and in the dim background the clergyman pointed out an elaborate apparatus for quickly altering the temperature of the air, and another for the rapid production of carbonic acid gas, since by means of a lens of carbonic acid gas sound can be refracted like light, and by changing the temperature of the air that conveys it, sound can be bent, also like a ray of light, in any desired direction. The whole cellar seemed in some way to sum up and synthesize the distinctive characteristics of the four rooms. Over it all, sheeting ceiling and walls, lay the living and receptive wax. Singularly suggestive, too, was the appearance of those huge metal discs, like lifeless, dark faces waiting the signal to open their bronze lips and cry aloud, ready for the advent of the Sound that should give them birth and force them to proclaim their mighty secret. Spinrobin stared, silent and fascinated, almost expecting them to begin there and then their dreadful and appalling music.

Yet the place was undeniably empty; no ghost of a sound stirred the gorgeous draperies; nothing but a faint metallic whispering seemed to breathe out from the big discs and forks and wires as Skale's voice, modulated and hushed though it was, vibrated gently against them. Nothing moved, nothing uttered, nothing lived—as yet.

"Destitute of all presence, you see it now," whispered the clergyman, shading the candle with one huge hand; "though before long, when we transfer our great captured syllable down here, you shall know it alive and singing with a thousand thunders. The Letters shall not escape me. The gongs and colours correspond exactly. They will retain both the sounds and the outlines... and the wax is sensitive as the heart of a child." And his big face shone quite dreadfully as the whole pomp and splendour of his dream come true set fire to his thoughts.

But Spinrobin was glad when at length they turned and moved slowly again up the stone steps and emerged into the pale December daylight. That dark cellar, wired, draped, waxed and be-gonged, awaiting its mighty occupant, filled his mind with too vast a sensation of wonder and anticipation for peace.

"And for the syllables to follow," Skale resumed when they were once more in the library, "we shall want spaces larger still. There are great holes in these hills"—stretching out an arm to indicate the mountains above the house—"and down yonder in the heart of those cliffs by the sounding sea there are caverns. They are far, but the distance is of no consequence. They will serve us well. I know them. I have marked them. They are ready."

He swept his beard to and fro with one hand. Spinrobin already saw those holes and caverns in the terms of sound and colour.

"And—for the entire name—when completed?" he asked, knowing that the question was but a feeble substitute for that other one he burned to ask, yet dared not allow his lips to utter. Skale turned and looked at him. He raised his hands aloft. His voice boomed again as of old.

"The open sky!" he cried with enthusiasm; "the vault of heaven itself! For no solid structure exists in the world, not even the ribs of these old hills, that could withstand the power of that—of that eternal and terrific—"

Spinrobin leapt to his feet. The question swept from his lips at last like a flame. Miriam clung to his arm, trying in vain to stop him.

"Then tell me," he cried aloud, "tell me, you great blasphemer, whose is the Name that you seek to utter under heaven... and tell me why it is my soul faints and is so fearfully afraid?"

Mr. Skale looked at him for a moment as a man might look at some trifling phenomenon of life that puzzled yet interested him. But there was love in his eyes—love, and the forgiveness of a great soul. Spinrobin, afraid at his own audacity, met his eyes recklessly, while Miriam peered from one to the other, perplexed and questioning.

"Spinrobin," said the clergyman at length, in a voice turned soft and tender with compassion, "the name I seek—this awful name we may all eventually utter together, completely formed—is one that no living man has spoken for nigh two thousand years, though all this time the search has been kept alive by a few men in every age and every country of the world. Some few, they say—ah, yes, '*they say*'—have found it, then instantly forgotten it again; for once pronounced it may not be retained, but goes utterly lost to the memory on the instant. Only once, so far as we may know"—he lowered his voice to a hushed and reverent whisper that thrilled about them in the air like the throbbing of a string—"has it been preserved: the Prophet of Nazareth, purer and simpler than all other men, recovered the correct utterance of the first two syllables, and swiftly—very swiftly—phonetically, too, of necessity,—wrote them down before the wondrous memory had time to fade; then sewed the piece of parchment into his thigh, and hence 'had Power' all his life.

"It is a name," he continued, his tone rising to something of its old thunder, "that sounds like the voice of many waters, that piles the ocean into standing heaps and makes the high hills to skip like little lambs. It is a name the ancient Hebrews concealed, as Tetragrammaton, beneath a thousand devices, the name, they said, that 'rusheth through the universe,' to call upon which—that is, to utter correctly—is to call upon that name which is far above all others that can be named—"

He paused midway in the growing torrent of his speech and lifted his companion out of the sofa. He set him upon his feet, holding both his hands and peering deep into his eyes—those bewildered yet unflinching blue eyes of the little man who sought terrific adventure as an escape from insignificance—

"—to know which," he added, in a sudden awed whisper, "is to know the ultimate secrets of life and death, and to read the riddle of the world and the soul—to become even as itself—Gods."

He stopped abruptly, and again that awful, flaming smile ran over his face, flushing it from chin to forehead with the power of his burning and tremendous belief.

Spinrobin was already weeping inwardly, without sound. He understood at last, only too well, what was coming. Skale's expression held the whole wild glory, and the whole impious audacity of what seemed his blasphemous spiritual discovery. The fires were alight in his eyes. He stooped down lower and opened wide his capacious arms. The next second, Spinrobin, Miriam, and Mrs. Mawle, who had unexpectedly come upon them from behind, were gathered all together against his breast. His voice then dropped suddenly to a tiny whisper of awful joy that seemed to creep from his lips like some message too mighty to be fully known, and half lost itself among the strands of his beard.

"My wonderful redeemed children, notes in my human chord," he whispered over their heads, "it is the Name that shall make us as God, for it is none other than the Name that rusheth through the universe"—his breath failed him most curiously for an instant—"the NAME OF THE ALMIGHTY!"

I

A certain struggling incoherence is manifest in Spinrobin's report of it all, as of a man striving to express violent thoughts in a language he has not yet mastered. It is evident, for instance, as those few familiar with the "magical" use of sound in ceremonial and the power that resides in "true naming" will realize, that he never fully understood Skale's intended use of the chord, or why this complex sound was necessary for the utterance of the complex "Name."

Moreover, the powers concealed in the mere letters, while they laid hold upon his imagination, never fully entered his understanding. Few minds, it seems, can conceive of any deity as other than some anthropomorphic extension of themselves, for the idea is too greatly blinding to admit human thought within a measurable distance even of a faintest conception. The true, stupendous nature of the forces these letters in the opening syllable clothed, Spinrobin unquestionably never apprehended. Miriam, with her naked and undefiled intuitions, due to utter ignorance of worldly things from birth, came nearer to the reality; but then Miriam was now daily more and more caught up into the vortex of a sweet and compelling human love, and in proportion as this grew she feared the great experiment that might—so Spinrobin had suggested—spell Loss. Gradually dread closed the avenues of her spirit that led so fearfully to Heaven; and in their place she saw the dear yet thorny paths that lay with Spinny upon the earth.

They no longer, these two bewildered loving children, spoke of one another in the far-fetched terminology of sound and music. He no longer called her his "brilliant little sound," nor did she respond with "you perfect echo"; they fell back—sign of a gradual concession to more human things—upon the gentler terminology, if the phrase may be allowed, of Winky. They shared Winky between them... though neither one nor other of them divined yet what Winky actually meant in their just-opening lives.

"Winky is yours," she would say, "because you made him, but he belongs to me too, because he simply can't live without me!"

"Or I without you, Little Magic," he whispered, laughing tenderly. "So, you see, we are all three together."

Her face grew slightly troubled.

"He only pays me visits, though. Sometimes I think you hide him, or tell him not to come." And far down in her deep grey eyes swam the first moisture of rising tears. "Don't you, my wonderful Spinny?"

"Sometimes I forget him, perhaps," he replied gravely, "but that is only when I think of what may be coming if—the experiment succeeds—"

"Succeeds?" she exclaimed. "You mean if it fails!" Her voice dropped instinctively, and they looked over their shoulders to make sure they were alone.

He came up very close to her and spoke in her small pink ear. "If it succeeds," he whispered, "we go to Heaven, I suppose; if it fails we stay upon the earth." Then he stood off, holding her hands at arm's length and gazing down upon her. "Do you want to go to Heaven?" he asked very deliberately, "or to stay here upon the earth with me and Winky—?"

She was in his arms the same second, laughing and crying with the strange conflict of new and inexplicable emotions.

"I want to be with you here, and forever. Heaven frightens me now. But—oh, Spinny, dear protecting thing, I want—I also want—" She broke off abruptly, and Spinrobin, unable to see her face buried against his shoulder, could not guess whether she was laughing or weeping. He only divined that something in her heart, profound as life itself, something she had never been warned to conceal, was clamouring for comprehension and satisfaction.

"Miriam, tell me exactly. I'm sure I shall understand—"

"I want Winky to be with us always—not only sometimes—on little visits," he heard between the broken breathing.

"I'll tell him—"

"But there's no good telling *him*," she interrupted almost fiercely, "it is *me* you must tell..."

Spinrobin's heart sank within him. She was in pain and he could not quite understand. He pressed her hard against him, keeping silence.

Presently she lifted her face from his coat, and he saw the tears of mingled pain and happiness in her eyes—the eyes of this girl-woman who knew not the common ugly standards of life because no woman had ever told them to her.

"You see, Winky is not really mine unless I have some share in making him too," she said very softly. "When I have made him too, then he will stay forever with us, I think."

And Spinrobin, beginning to understand, knowing within him that singular exultation of triumphant love which comes to a pure man when he meets the mother-to-be of his firstborn, lowered his own face very reverently to hers, and kissed her on the cheeks and eyes—saying nothing, and vaguely wondering whether the awful name that Skale sought with so much thunder and lightning, did not lie at that very moment, sweetly singing its divinest message, between the contact of this pair of youthful lips, the lips of himself and Miriam.

II

And Philip Skale, meanwhile, splendid and independent of all common obstacles, thundered along his tempestuous mad way, regardless and ignorant of all signs of disaffection. The rest of that week—a week of haunting wonder and beauty—was devoted to the carrying out of the strange programme. It is not possible to tell in detail the experience of each separate room. Spinrobin does it, yet only succeeds in repeating himself; and, as has been seen, his powers failed even in that first chamber of awe. The language does not exist in which adventures so remote from normal experience can be clothed without straining the mind to the verge of the unintelligible. It appears, however, that each room possessed its colour, note and form, which later were to issue forth and combine in the even vaster pattern, chord and outline which should include them all.

Even the thought of it strained the possibilities of belief and the resources of the imagination... His soul fluttered and shrank.

They continued the processes of prayer and fasting Skale had ordained as the time for the experiment drew near, and the careful vibratory utterance of the "word" belonging to each room, the vibrations of which threw their inner selves into a condition of safe—or comparatively safe—receptivity. But Spinrobin no longer said his prayers, for the thought that soon he was to call upon the divine and mighty name in reality prevented his doing so in the old way of childhood—nominally. He feared there might come an answer.

He literally walked the dizzy edge of precipices that dropped over the edge of the world. The incoherence of all this traffic with sound and name had always bewildered him, even to the point of darkness, whereas now it did more, it appalled him in some sense that was monstrous and terrifying. Yet, while weak with terror when he tried to face the possible results, and fevered with the notion of entering some new condition (even though one of glory) where Miriam might no longer be as he now knew her, it was the savage curiosity he felt that prevented his coming to a definite decision and telling Mr. Skale that he withdrew from the whole affair.

Then the idea grew in his mind that the clergyman was obsessed by some perverted spiritual force, some "Devil" who deceived him, and that the name he sought to pronounce was after all not good—not God. His thoughts, fears, hopes, all became hopelessly entangled, through them one thing alone holding clear and steady—the passionate desire to keep Miriam as she was now, and to be with her forever. His mind played tricks with him too. Day and night the house echoed with new sounds; the very walls grew resonant; the entire building, buried away among these desolate hills, trembled as though he were imprisoned within the belly of some monstrous and gigantic fiddle.

Mr. Skale, too, began to change, it seemed. While physically he increased, as it were, with the power of his burning enthusiasm, his beard longer and more ragged, his eyes more luminous, and his voice shaking through the atmosphere almost like wind, his personality, in some curious fashion, seemed at the same time to retire and become oddly tinged with a certain remoteness from reality. Spinrobin once or twice caught himself wondering if he were not after all some legendary or pagan figure, some mighty character of dream or story, and that presently he, Spinrobin, would awake and write down the most wonderful vision the world had ever known. His imagination, it will be seen, was affected in more ways than one...

With a tremendous earnestness the clergyman went about the building, down the long dark corridors and across the halls, his long soft strides took him swiftly everywhere; his mere presence charged with some potent force that betrayed itself in the fire of his eyes and the flush of his cheeks.

Spinrobin thought of him as some daring blasphemer, knocking at a door in the sky. The sound of that knocking ran all about the universe. And when the door opened, the heavens would roll back like an enormous, flat curtain...

"Any moment almost," Skale whispered to him, smiling, "the day may be upon us. Keep yourself ready—and—in tune."

And Spinrobin, expecting a thunderclap in his sleep, but ever plucky, answered in his high-pitched voice, "I'm ready, Mr. Philip Skale, I'm ready! I'm game too!" when, truthfully speaking, perhaps, he was neither one nor other.

He would start up from sleep in the nighttime at the least sound, and the roar of the December gales about the house became voices of portent that conveyed far more than the mere rushing of inarticulate winds...

"When the hour comes—and it is close at hand—we shall not fail to know it," said Skale, pallid with excitement. "The Letters will be out upon us. They will live! But with an intense degree of exuberant life far beyond what we know as life—we, in our puny, sense-limited bodies!" And the scorn in his voice came from the centre of his heart. "For what we hear as sound is only a section," he cried, "only a section of sound-vibrations—as they exist."

"The vibrations our ears can take are *very* small, I know," interpolated Spinrobin, cold at heart, while Miriam, hiding behind chairs and tables that offered handy protection, watched with mingled anxiety and confidence, knowing that in the last resort her adorable and "wonderful Spinny" would guide her aright. Love filled her heart, ousting that other portentous Heaven!

III

And then Skale announced that the time was ready for rehearsals.

"Let us practise the chord," he said, "so that when the moment comes suddenly upon us, in the twinkling of an eye, in the daytime or in the night, we shall be prepared, and each shall fly to his appointed place and utter his appointed note."

The reasons for these definite arrangements he did not pretend to explain, for they belonged to a part of his discovery that he kept rigidly to himself; and why Spinrobin and Miriam were to call their notes from the corridor itself, while Skale boomed his great bass in the prepared cellar, Mrs. Mawle chanting her alto midway in the hall, acting as a connecting channel in some way, was apparently never made fully clear. In Spinrobin's imagination it was very like a practical illustration of the written chord, the notes rising from the bass clef to the high soprano—the cellar to the attic, so to speak. But, whatever the meaning behind it, Skale was exceedingly careful to teach to each of them his and her appointed place.

"When the Letters move of themselves, and make the first sign," he repeated, "we shall know it beyond all doubt or question. At any moment of the day or night it may come. Each of you then hasten to your appointed place and wait for the sound of my bass in the cellar. There will be no mistake about it; you will hear it rising through the building. Then, each in turn, as it reaches you, lift your voices and call your notes. The chord thus rising through the building will gather in the flying Letters: it will unite them; it will summon them down to the fundamental master-tone I utter in the cellar. The moment the Letter summoned by each particular voice reaches the cellar, that voice must cease its utterance. Thus, one by one, the four mighty Letters will come to rest below. The gongs will vibrate in sympathetic resonance; the colours will tremble and respond; the finely drawn wires will link the two, and the lens of gas will lead them to the wax, and the record of the august and terrible syllable will be completely chained. At any desired moment afterwards I shall be able to reawaken it. Its phonetic utterance, its correct pronunciation, captured thus in the two media of air and ether, sound and light, will be in my safe possession, ready for use.

"But"—and he looked down upon his listeners with a dreadful and impressive gravity that yet only just concealed the bursting exultation the thought caused him to feel—"remember that once you have uttered your note, you will have sucked out from the Letter a portion of its own terrific life and force, which will immediately pass into yourself. You will instantly absorb this, for you will have called upon a mighty name—the mightiest—and your prayer will have been answered." He stooped and whispered as in an act of earnest prayer, *"We shall be as Gods!"*

Something of cold splendour, terribly possessing, came close to them as he spoke the words; for this was no empty phrase. Behind it lay the great drive of a relentless reality. And it struck at the very root of the fear that grew every moment more insistent in the hearts of the two lovers. They did not want to become as gods. They desired to remain quietly human and to *love*!

But before either of them could utter speech, even had they dared, the awful clergyman continued; and nothing brought home to them more vividly the horrible responsibility of the experiment, and the results of possible failure, than the few words with which he concluded.

"And to mispronounce, to utter falsely, to call inaccurately, will mean to summon into life upon the world—and into the heart of the utterer—that which is incomplete, that which is not God—Devils!—devils of that subtle Alteration which is destruction—the devils of a Lie."

*

And so for hours at a time they rehearsed the sounds of the chord, but very softly, lest the sound should rise and reach the four rooms and invite the escape of the waiting Letters prematurely.

Mrs. Mawle, holding the bit of paper on which her instructions were clearly written, was as eager almost as her master, and as the note she had to utter was practically the only one left in the register of her voice, her deafness provided little difficulty.

"Though when the letters awake into life and cry aloud," said Skale, beaming upon her dear old apple-skinned face, "it will be in tones that even the deaf shall hear. For they will spell a measure of redemption that shall destroy in a second of time all physical disabilities whatsoever..."

It was at this moment Spinrobin asked a question that for days had been hovering about his lips. He asked it gravely, hesitatingly, even solemnly, while Miriam hung upon the answer with an anxiety as great as his own.

"And if any one of us fails," he said, "and pronounces falsely, will the result affect all of us, or only the utterer?"

"The utterer only," replied the clergyman. "For it is his own spirit that must absorb the forces and powers invoked by the sound he utters."

He took the question lightly, it seemed. The possibility of failure was too remote to be practical.

I

But Spinrobin was hardly prepared for the suddenness of the denouement. He had looked for a longer period of preparation, with the paraphernalia of a considerable, even an august ceremony. Instead, the announcement came with an abrupt simplicity that caught him with a horrid shock of surprise. He was taken wholly unawares.

"The only thing I fear," Mr. Skale had confided to them, "is that the vibrations of our chord may have already risen to the rooms and cause a premature escape. But, even so, we shall have ample warning. For the deaf, being protected from the coarser sounds of earth, are swift to hear the lightest whispers from Heaven. Mrs. Mawle will know. Mrs. Mawle will instantly warn us…"

And this, apparently, was what happened, though not precisely as Mr. Skale had intended, nor with the margin for preparation he had hoped. It was all so swift and brief and shattering, that to hear Spinrobin tell it makes one think of a mass of fireworks that some stray spark has sent with blazing explosion into the air, to the complete loss of the calculated effect had they gone off seriatim as intended.

And in the awful stress of excitement there can be no question that Spinny acted out of that subconscious region of the mind which considers and weighs deeds before passing them on to the surface mind, translating them into physical expression and thinking itself responsible for the whole operation. The course he adopted was thus instinctive, and, since he had no time to judge, blameless.

Neither he nor Miriam had any idea really that their minds, subconsciously, were already made up. Yet only that morning he had been talking with her, skirting round the subject as they always did, ashamed of his doubts about success, and trying to persuade her, and, therefore, himself, that the path of duty lay in following their leader blindly to the very end.

He had seen her on the stairs ahead of him, and had overtaken her quickly. He drew her down beside him, and they sat like two children perched on the soft-carpeted steps.

"It's coming, you know," he said abruptly, "the moment's getting very close."

He felt the light shudder that passed through her into himself. She turned her face to him and he saw the flush of excitement painted in the centre of the usually pale cheeks. He thought of some rare flower, delicately exotic, that had sprung suddenly into blossom from the heart of the bleak December day, out of the very boards whereon they sat.

"We shall then be as gods," he added, "filled with the huge power of those terrific Letters. And that is only the beginning." In himself he was striving to coax a fading enthusiasm, and to pour it into her. Her little hand stole into his. "We shall be a sort of angel together, I suppose. Just think of it...!" His voice was not as thrilling as it ought to have been, for very human notes vibrated down below in the part he tried to keep back. He saw the flush fade from her cheeks, and the pallor spread. "You and I, Miriam—something tremendous together, greater than any other man and woman in the whole world. Think of it, dear baby; just think of it...!"

A tiny frown gathered upon her forehead, darkening the grey eyes with shadows.

"But—lose our Winky!" she said, nestling against his coat, her voice singularly soft, her fingers scratching gently the palm of his hand where they lay.

"Hush, hush!" he answered, kissing her into silence. "We must have more faith. I think everything will be all right. And there is no reason why we should lose our Winky," he added, very tenderly, smothering the doubt as best he could, "although we may find his name changed. Like the rest of us, he will get a 'new name' I suppose."

"Then he won't be *our* Winky any longer," she objected, with a touch of obstinacy that was very seductive. "We shall all be different. Perhaps we shall be too wonderful to need each other any more... Oh, Spinny, you precious thing my life needs, think of that! We may be too wonderful even to care!"

Spinrobin turned and faced her. He tried to speak with authority and conviction, but he was a bad actor always. He met her soft grey eyes, already moist and shining with a tenderness of love beyond belief, and gazed into them with what degree of sternness he could.

"Miriam," he said solemnly, "is it possible that you do not want us to be as gods?"

Her answer came this time without hesitation. His pretended severity only made her happy, for nothing could intimidate by a hair's breadth this exquisite first love of her awakening soul.

"Some day, perhaps, oh, my sweet Master," she whispered with trembling lips, "but not now. I want to be on earth first with you—and with our Winky."

To hear that precious little voice call him "sweet Master" was almost more than he could bear. He made an effort, however, to insist upon this fancied idea of "duty" to Skale; though everything, of course, betrayed him—eyes, voice, gestures.

"But we owe it to Mr. Skale to become as gods," he faltered, trying to make the volume of his voice atone for its lack of conviction.

And it was then she uttered the simple phrase that utterly confounded him, and showed him the new heaven and new earth wherein he and she and Winky already lived.

"I am as God *now*," she said simply, the whole passion of a clean, strong little soul behind the words. "You have made me so! You love me!"

II

The same moment, before they could speak or act, Skale was upon them from behind with a roar.

"Practising your splendid notes together!" he cried, thundering down the steps past them, three at a time, clothed for the first time in the flowing scarlet robe he usually wore only in the particular room where his own "note" lived. "That's capital! Sing it together in your hearts and in your souls and in your minds; and the more the better!"

He swept by them like a storm, vanishing through the hall below like some living flame of fire. They both understood that he wore that robe for protection, and that throughout the house the heralds of the approaching powers of the imprisoned Letters were therefore already astir. His steps echoed below them in the depths of the building as he descended to the cellar, intent upon some detail of the appalling consummation that drew every minute nearer.

They turned and faced one another, breathless a little. Tenderness and terror shone plainly in their eyes, but Spinrobin, ever an ineffectual little man, and with nothing of the "Master" really in his composition anywhere, found no word to speak. That sudden irruption of the terrific clergyman into their intimate world had come with an effect of dramatic and incalculable authority. Like a blast of air that drives the furnace to new heat and turns the metal white, his mind now suddenly saw clear and sure. The effect of the incident was too explosive, however, for him to find expression. Action he found in a measure, but no words. He took Miriam passionately into his arms as they stood there in the gathering dusk upon the staircase of that haunted and terrible building, and Miriam it was who found the words upon which they separated and went quietly away to the solitude each needed for the soul.

"We'll leave the gods alone," she said with gentle decision, yet making it seem as though she appealed to his greater strength and wisdom to decide; "I want nothing but you—you and Winky. And all you really want is me."

But in his room he heard the vibrations of the clergyman's voice rising up through the floor and walls as he practised in the cellar the sounds with which the ancient Hebrews concealed the Tetragrammaton: Yod—He—Vau—He: Jehovah—Jahve—of which the approaching great experiment, however, concerned itself only with the opening vibrations of the first letter—Yod...

And, as he listened, he hesitated again... wondering after all whether Miriam was right.

III

It was towards the end of their short silent dinner that very night—the silence due to the fact that everybody was intently listening—when Spinrobin caught the whisper of a singular faint sound that he took first to be the rising of wind. The wind sometimes came down that way with curious gulps from the terraces of the surrounding moors. Yet in this sound was none of that rush and sigh that the hills breed. It did not drop across the curves of the world; it rose from the centre.

He looked up sharply, then at once realized that the sound was not outside at all, but inside—inside the very room where he sat facing Skale and Miriam. Then something in his soul recognized it. It was the first wave in an immense vibration.

Something stretched within him as foam stretches on the elastic side of a heaped Atlantic roller, retreated, then came on again with a second gigantic crest. The rhythm of the huge sound had caught him. The life in him expanded awfully, rose to far summits, dropped to utter depths. A sense of glowing exaltation swept through him as though wings of power lifted his heart with enormous ascendancy. The biggest passions of his soul stirred—the sweetest dreams, yearnings, aspirations he had ever known were blown to fever heat. Above all, his passion for Miriam waxed tumultuous and possessed him.

Mr. Skale dropped his fruit knife and uttered a cry, but a cry of so peculiar a character that Spinrobin thought for a moment he was about to burst into song. At the same instant he stood up, and his chair fell backwards with a crash upon the floor. Spinrobin stood up too. He asserts always that he was lifted up. He recognized no conscious effort of his own. It was at this point, moreover, that Miriam, pale as linen, yet uttering no sound and fully mistress of herself, left her side of the table and ran round swiftly to the protection of her lover.

She came close up. "Spinny," she said, "it's come!"

Thus all three were standing round that dinner table on the verge of some very vigorous action not yet disclosed, as people, vigilant and alert, stand up at a cry of fire, when the door from the passage opened noisily and in rushed Mrs. Mawle, surrounded by an atmosphere of light such as might come from a furnace door suddenly thrown wide in some dark foundry. Only the light was not steady; it was whirling.

She ran across the floor as though dancing—the dancing of a child—propelled, it seemed, by an irresistible drive of force behind;

while with her through the opened door came a roaring volume of sound that was terrible as Niagara let loose, yet at the same time exquisitely sweet, as birds or children singing. Upon these two incongruous qualities Spinrobin always insists.

"The deaf shall hear—!" came sharply from the clergyman's lips, the sentence uncompleted, for the housekeeper cut him short.

"They're out!" she cried with a loud, half-frightened jubilance; "Mr. Skale's prisoners are bursting their way about the house. And one of them," she added with a scream of joy and terror mingled, "is in my throat...!"

If the odd phrase she made use of stuck vividly in Spinrobin's memory, the appearance she presented impressed him even more. For her face was shining and alight, radiant as when Skale had called her true name weeks before. Flashes of flame-like beauty ran about the eyes and mouth; and she looked eighteen—eternally eighteen—with a youth that was permanent and unchanging. Moreover, not only was hearing restored to her, but her left arm, withered for years, was in the act of pointing to the ceiling, instinct with vigorous muscular life. Her whole presentment was splendid, intense—redeemed.

"The deaf hear!" repeated Skale in a shout, and was across the room with the impetus of a released projectile. "The Letters are out and alive! To your appointed places! The syllable has caught us! Quick, quick! If you love your soul and truth... fly!"

Deafening thunders rushed and crashed and blew about the room, interpenetrated everywhere at the same time by that searching strain of sweetness Spinrobin had first noticed. The sense of life, running free and abundant, was very remarkable. The same moment he found his hand clasped, and felt himself torn along by the side of the rushing clergyman into the hall. Behind them "danced" Mrs. Mawle, her cap awry, her apron flying, her elastic-side boots taking the light, dancing step of youth. With quick, gliding tread Miriam, still silent, was at his heels. He remembers her delicate, strange perfume reaching him faintly through all the incredible turmoil of that impetuous exit.

In the hall the roar increased terrifically about his ears. Skale, in his biggest booming voice, was uttering the names of Hebrew "angels"—invoking forces, that is, to his help; and behind him Mrs. Mawle was singing—singing fragments apparently of the "note" she had to utter, as well as fragments of her own "true name" thus magically recovered. Her restored arm gyrated furiously, her tripping youth spelt witchery. Yet the whole madness of the scene came to Spinrobin with a freezing wind of terror; for about it was a lawless, audacious blasphemy, that must surely win for itself a quite appalling punishment...

Yet nothing happened at once—nothing destructive, at least. Skale and the housekeeper, he saw, were hurriedly robing themselves in the red and yellow surplices that hung from nails in the hall, and the instinct to laugh at the sight was utterly overwhelmed when he remembered that these were the colours which were used for safety in their respective "rooms."... It was a scene of wild confusion and bewilderment which the memory refuses to reproduce coherently. In his own throat already began a passionate rising of sound that he knew was the "note" he had to utter attempting to escape, summoned forth automatically by these terrible vibrating Letters in the air. A cataract of sound seemed to fill the building and made it shake to its very foundations.

But the hall, he saw, was not only alive with "music," it was ablaze with light—a white and brilliant glory that at first dazzled him to the point of temporary blindness.

The same second Mr. Skale's voice, storming its way somehow above the tumult, made itself heard:

"To the rooms upstairs, Spinrobin! To the corridor with Miriam! And when you hear my voice from the cellar—*utter*! We may yet be in time to unite the Letters...!"

He released the secretary's hand, flinging it from him, and was off with a bounding, leaping motion like an escaped animal towards the stone passage that led to the cellar steps; and Spinrobin, turning about himself like a top in a perfect frenzy of bewilderment, heard his great voice as he disappeared round the corner:

"It has come upon me like a thief in the night! Before I am fully prepared it has called me! May the powers of the Name have mercy upon my soul...!" And he was gone. For the last time had Spinrobin set his eyes upon the towering earthly form of the Rev. Philip Skale.

IV

Then, at first, it seems, the old enthusiasm caught him, and with him, therefore, caught Miriam, too. That savage and dominant curiosity to know clutched him, overpowering even the assaults of a terror that fairly battered him. Through all the chaos and welter of his dazed mind he sought feverishly for the "note" he had to utter, yet found it not, for he was too horribly confused. Fiddles, sand-patterns, coloured robes, gongs, giant tuning-forks, wax-sheeted walls, aged-faces-turned-young and caverns-by-the-sea jostled one another in his memory with a jumble of disproportion quite inextricable.

Next, impelled by that driving sense of duty to Skale, he turned to the girl at his side: "Can you do it?" he cried.

Unable to make her voice heard above the clamour she nodded quickly in acquiescence. Spinrobin noticed that her little mouth was set rather firmly, though there was a radiance about her eyes and features that made her sweetly beautiful. He remembers that her loveliness and her pluck uplifted him above all former littlenesses of hesitation; and, seizing her outstretched hand, they flew up the main staircase and in less than a minute reached the opening of the long corridor where the rooms were.

Here, however, they stopped with a gasp, for a hurricane of moving air met them in the face like the draught from some immense furnace. Again the crest of a wave in the colossal sound-vibration had caught them. Staggering against the wall, they tried again and again to face the tempest of sound and light, but the space beyond them was lit with the same unearthly brilliance as the hall, and out of the whole long throat of that haunted corridor issued such a passion of music and such a torrent of gorgeous colour, that it seemed impossible for any aggregation of physical particles—least of all poor human bodies—to remain coherent for a single instant before the concentrated onslaught.

Yet, game to the inmost core of his little personality, and raised far above his normal powers by the evidence of Miriam's courage and fidelity, he struggled with all his might and searched through the chambers of his being for the note he was ordained to utter in the chord. The ignominy of failure, now that the great experiment was full upon him—failure in Miriam's eyes, too—was simply impossible to contemplate. Yet, in spite of every effort, the memory of that all-important note escaped him utterly, for the forces of his soul floundered, helpless and dishevelled, before the too mighty splendours that were upon him at such close quarters. The sounds he actually succeeded in emitting between dry and quivering lips were pitiful and feeble beyond words.

Down that living corridor, meanwhile, he saw the doors of the four rooms were gone, consumed like tissue paper; and through the narrow portals there shouldered forward, bathed in light ineffable, the separate outlines of the Letters so long imprisoned in inactivity. And with their appearance the sounds instantly ceased, having overpassed the limits of what is audible to human ears. A great stillness dropped about them with an abrupt crash of utter silence. For a "crash" of silence it was—all-shattering.

And then, from the categories of the incomprehensible and unmanifest, "something" loomed forth towards them where, limp and shaking, they leaned against the wall, and they witnessed the indescribable operation by which the four Letters, whirling and alive, ran together and melted into a single terrific semblance of a FORM... the sight of which entered the heart of Spinrobin and threatened to split it asunder with the joy of the most sublime terror and adoration a human soul has ever known.

And the whole gigantic glory of Skale's purpose came upon him like a tempest. The magnificent effrontery by which the man sought to storm his way to heaven again laid its spell upon him. The reaction was of amazing swiftness. It almost seemed as though time ceased to operate, so instantaneously did his mood pass from terror to elation— wild, ecstatic elation that could dare anything and everything to share in the awful delight and wonder of Skale's transcendent experiment.

And so, forgetting himself and his little disabilities of terror and shrinking, he sought once again for the note he was to utter in the chord. And this time he found it.

V

Very faintly, yet distinctly audible in the deep stillness, it sounded far away down in the deeps of his being. And, with a splendid spiritual exultation tearing and swelling in his heart, he turned at once triumphantly to Miriam beside him.

"Utter your note too!" he cried. "Utter it with mine, for any moment now we shall hear the command from the cellar... Be ready...!"

And the FORM, meanwhile, limned in the wonder of an undecipherable or at least untranslatable geometry, silently roaring, enthroned in the undiscoverable colours beyond the spectrum, swept towards them as he spoke.

At the same instant Miriam answered him, her exquisite little face set like a rock, her marble pallor painted with the glory of the approaching splendours. Just when the moment of success was upon them; when the flying Letters were abroad; when all the difficult weeks of preparation were face to face with the consummation; and when any moment Skale's booming bass might rise from the bowels of the building as the signal to utter the great chord and unite the fragments of the first divine syllable; when Spinrobin had at last conquered his weakness and recovered his note—then, at this decisive and supreme moment, Miriam asserted herself and took the reins of command.

"No," she said, looking with sudden authority straight into his eyes, "no! I will not utter the note. Nor shall you utter yours!" And she clapped her little hand tight upon his mouth.

In that instant of unutterable surprise the two great forces of his life and personality met together with an explosive violence wholly beyond his power to control. For on the one hand lay the fierce enticement of Skale's heaven, with all that it portended, and on the other the deep though temporarily submerged human passion of his love for the girl. Miriam's sudden action revealed the truth to him better than any argument. In a flash he realized that her choice was made, and that she was in entire and final revolt against the whole elaborate experiment and all that it involved. The risk of losing her Spinny, or finding him changed in some condition of redemption where he would no longer be the little human thing she so dearly loved, had helped her to this final, swift conclusion.

With her hand tight over his lips, and her face of white decision before him, he understood. She called him with those big grey eyes to the sweet and common uses of life, instead of to the heights of some audacious heaven where they might be as gods with Philip Skale. She clung to humanity. And Spinrobin, seeing her at last with spiritual eyes fully opened, knew finally that she was right.

"But oh," he always cries, "in that moment I knew the most terrible choice I have ever had to make, for it was not a choice between life and death, but a choice between two lives, each of infinite promised wonder. And what do you think it was that decided me, and made me choose the wholesome, humble life with little Miriam in preference to the grandeur of Skale's vast dream? What *do* you think?" And his face always turns pink and then flame-coloured as he asks it, hesitating absurdly before giving the answer. "I'll tell you, because you'd never guess in this world." And then he lowers his voice and says, "It was the delicious little sweet perfume of her fingers as she held them over my lips...!"

That delicate, faint smell was the symbol of human happiness, and through all the whirlwind of sound and colour about him, it somehow managed to convey its poignant, searching message of the girl's utter love straight into his heart. Thus curiously out of proportion and insignificant, indeed, are sometimes the decisive details that in moments of overwhelming experience turn the course of life's river this way or that...

With a single wild cry in his soul that found no audible expression, he gave up the unequal struggle. He turned, and with Miriam by his side, flew down the corridor from the advent of the Immensity that was upon them—from the approach of the escaping Letters.

VI

How Spinrobin found his way out of that sound-stricken house remains an unsolved mystery. He never understood it himself; he remembers only that when they reached the ground floor the vibrations of Skale's opening bass note had already begun. Its effect, too, was immediately noticeable. For the roar of the escaping Letters, which upstairs had reached so immense a volume as to be recognized only in terms of silence, now suddenly grew in a measure harnessed and restrained. Their vibration became reduced—down closer to the sixteen-foot wavelength which is the limit of human audition. They were being leashed in by the summoning master-tone. They grew once more audible.

On the rising swirl of sound the two humans were swept down passages and across halls, as two leaves are borne by a tempest, and after frantic efforts, in which Spinrobin bruised his body against doors and walls without number, he found himself at last in the open air, and at a considerable distance from the house of terror. Stars shone overhead. He saw the outline of hills. Breaths of cool wind fanned his burning skin and eyes.

But he dared not turn to look or listen. The music of that opening note, now rising through the building from the cellar, might catch him and win him back. The chord in which himself and Miriam were to have uttered their appointed tones, even half-told, was still mighty to overwhelm. Its effect upon the Letters themselves had been immediate.

The feeling that he had proved faithless to Skale, unworthy of the great experiment, never properly attuned to this fearful music of the gods—this was forgotten in the overmastering desire to escape from it all into the safety of common human things with Miriam. Setting his course ever up the hills, he ran on and on, till breath failed him utterly and he was obliged to stop for lack of strength. And it was only then he realized that the whole time the girl had been in his arms. He had been carrying her.

Placing her on the ground, he caught a glimpse of her eyes in the darkness, and saw that they were still charged with the one devouring passion that had made the sacrifice of Skale and of all her training since birth inevitable. Soft and glowing with her first knowledge of love, her grey eyes shone like stars newly risen.

"Come, come!" he whispered hoarsely; "we must get as far as possible—away from it all. Across the hills we shall find safety. Once the splendours overtake us we are lost..."

Seizing her by the hand, they pressed on again, the ocean of sound rising and thundering behind them and below.

Without knowing it, he had taken the path by which the clergyman had brought him from the station weeks ago on the day of his first arrival. With a confused memory, as of a dream, he recognized it. The ground was slippery with dead leaves whose odour penetrated sharply the air of night. Everywhere about him, as they paused from time to time in the little open spaces, the trees pressed up thickly; and ever from the valley they had just left the increasing tide of sound came pouring up after them like the roar of the sea escaping through doors upon the surface of the world.

And even now the marvellous, enticing wonder of it caught him more than once and made him hesitate. The sense of what he was giving up sickened him with a great sudden yearning of regret. The mightiness of that loved leader, lonely and unafraid, trafficking with the principalities and powers of sound, and reckoning without misgiving upon the cooperation of his other "notes"—this plucked fearfully at his heartstrings. But only in great tearing gusts, so to speak, which passed the instant he realized the little breathless, grey-eyed girl at his side, charged with her beautiful love for him and the wholesome ambition for human things.

"Oh! but the heaven we're losing...!" he cried once aloud, unable to contain himself. "Oh, Miriam... and I have proved unworthy... small...!"

"Small enough to stay with me forever and ever... here on the earth," she replied passionately, seizing his hand and drawing him further up the hill. Then she stopped suddenly and gathered a handful of dead leaves, moss, twigs and earth. The exquisite familiar perfume as she held it to his face pierced through him with a singular power of conviction.

"We should lose *this*," she exclaimed; "there's none of this... in heaven! The earth, the earth, the dear, beautiful earth, with you... and Winky... is what I want!"

And when he stopped her outburst with a kiss, fully understanding the profound truth she so quaintly expressed, he smelt the trees and mountains in her hair, and her fragrance was mingled there with the fragrance of that old earth on which they stood.

VII

The rising flood of sound sent them charging ahead the same minute, for it seemed upon them with a rush; and it was only after much stumbling and floundering among trees and boulders that they emerged into the open space of the hills beyond the woods. Actually, perhaps, they had been running for twenty minutes, but to them it seemed that they had been running for days. They stood still and looked about them.

"You shall never regret, never, never," Miriam whispered quickly. "I can make you happier than all this ever could," and she waved her arm towards the house below. "And you know it, my little Master."

But before he could reply, or do more than place an arm about her waist to support her, something came to pass that communicated its message to their souls with an incalculable certainty neither could explain. Perhaps it was that distance enabled them to distinguish between the sounds more clearly, or perhaps their beings were still so intimately connected with Skale that some psychic warning travelled up to them across the night; but at any rate there then came about this sharp and sudden change in the quality of the sound-tempest round them that proclaimed the arrival of an exceedingly dramatic moment. The nature of the rushing, flying vibrations underwent alteration. And, looking one another in the eyes, they realized what it meant.

"He's beginning…" faltered Spinrobin in some skeleton of a voice. "Skale has begun to *utter*…!" He said it beneath his breath.

Down in the cellar of that awful house the giant clergyman, alone and undismayed, had begun to call the opening vibration of the living chord which was to gather in this torrent of escaping Letters and unite them in temporary safety in the crypts of the prepared vault. For the first time in eighteen hundred years the initial sound of the "Name that rusheth through the universe"—the first sound of its opening syllable, that is—was about to thunder its incalculable message over the earth.

Crouching close against each other they stood there on the edge of the woods, the night darkly smothering about them, the bare, open hills lying beyond in the still sky, waiting for the long-apprehended climax—the utterance of the first great syllable.

"It will make him… as God," crashed the thought through Spinrobin's brain as he experienced the pangs of the fiercest remorse he had ever known. "Even without our two notes the power will be sublime…!"

But, through Miriam's swiftly-beating heart, as she pressed closer and closer: "I know your true name… and you are mine. What else in heaven or earth can ever matter…?"

I

Skale had indeed begun to utter. And to these two bewildered children standing there alone with their love upon the mountain, it seemed that the whole world knew.

Those desolate hills that rolled away like waves beneath the stars; the whispering woods about them; the distant sea, eternally singing its own note of sadness; the boulders at their feet; the very stars themselves, listening in the heart of night—one and all were somehow aware that a portion of the great Name which first called them into being was about to issue from the sleep of ages once again into manifestation... Perhaps to quicken them into vaster life, perhaps to change their forms, perhaps to merge them all back into the depths of the original "word" of creation... with the roar of a dissolving universe...

Through everything, from the heart of the hidden primroses below the soil to the centre of the huge moors above, there ran some swift thrill of life as the sounds of which they were the visible expression trembled in sympathetic resonance with the opening vibrations of the great syllable.

Philip Skale had begun to utter. Alone in the cellar of that tempest-stricken house, already aware probably that the upper notes of his chord had failed him, he was at last in the act of calling upon the Name that Rusheth through the Universe... the syllable whose powers should pass into his own being and make him as the gods...

And, first of all, to the infinite surprise of these two listening, shaking lovers, the roaring thunders that had been battling all about them, grew faint and small, and then dropped away into mere trickles of sound, retreating swiftly down into the dark valley where the house stood, as though immense and invisible leashes drew them irresistibly back. One by one the Letters fled away, leaving only a murmur of incredibly sweet echoes behind them in the hills, as the master-sound, spoken by this fearless and audacious man, gathered them into their appointed places in the cellar.

But if they expected stupendous things to follow they were at first singularly disappointed. For, instead of woe and terror, instead of the foundering of the visible universe, there fell about the listening world a cloak of the most profound silence they had ever known, soft beyond conception. The Name was not in the whirlwind. Out of the heart of that deathly stillness it came—a small, sweet voice, that was undeniably the voice of Philip Skale, its awful thunders all smoothed away. With it, too, like a faint overtone, came the yet gentler music of another voice. The bass and alto were uttering their appointed notes in harmony and without dismay.

Everywhere the sound rose up through the darkness of great distance, yet at the same time ran most penetratingly sweet, close beside them in their very ears. So magically intimate indeed was it, yet so potentially huge for all its soft beginning, that Spinrobin declares that what he heard was probably not the actual voices, but only some high liberated harmonics of them.

The sounds, moreover, were not distinguishable as consonants and vowels in the ordinary sense, and to this day remain for him beyond all reach of possible reproduction. He did not hear them as "word" or "syllable," but as some incalculably splendid Message that was too mighty to be taken in, yet at the same time was sweeter than all imagined music, simple as a little melody "sweetly sung in tune," artless as wind through rustling branches.

And, moreover, as this small, sweet voice ran singing everywhere about them in the darkness of hills and woods, Spinrobin realized, with a whole revolution of wonder sweeping through him, that the sound, for all its gentleness, was at work vehemently upon the surface of the landscape, altering and shifting the pattern of the solid earth, just as the sand had wreathed into outlines at the sound of his own voice weeks ago, and as the form of the clergyman had changed at the vibrations of the test night.

The first letters of the opening syllable of this divine and magical name were passing over the world... shifting the myriad molecules that composed it by the stress and stir of its vast harmonics... changing the pattern.

But this time the change was not dreadful; the new outline, even before he actually perceived it, was beautiful above all known forms of beauty. The outer semblance of the old earth appeared to melt away and reveal that heart of clean and dazzling wonder which burns ever at its inmost core—the naked spirit divined by poets and mystics since the beginning of time. It was a new heaven and a new earth that pulsed below them in response to the majesty of this small sweet voice. All nature knew, from the birds that started out of sleep into passionate singing, to the fish that stirred in the depths of the sea, and the wild deer that sprang alert in their wintry coverts, scenting an eternal spring. For the earth rolled up as a scroll, shaking the outworn skin of centuries from her face, and suffering all her rocky structure to drop away and disclose the soft and glowing loveliness of an actual being—a being most tenderly and exquisitely alive. It was the beginning of spiritual vision in their own hearts. The name had set them free. The blind saw—a part of God...

II

And then, in Spinrobin's heart, the realization of failure—that he was not in his appointed place, following his great leader to the stars, clashed together with the splendour of his deep and simple love for this trembling slip of a girl beside him.

The thought that God, as it were, had called him and he had been afraid to run and answer to his name overpowered his timid, aching soul with such a flood of emotion that he found himself struggling with a glorious temptation to tear down the mountainside again to the house and play his appointed part—utter his note in the chord even thus late. For the essential bitterness and pain that lies at the heart of all transitory earthly things—the gnawing sense of incompleteness and vanity that touches the section of transitory existence men call "life," met face to face with this passing glimpse of reality, timeless and unconditioned, which the sound of the splendid name flashed so terrifically before his awakened soul-vision,—and threatened to overwhelm him.

In another instant he would have yielded and gone; forgotten even Miriam, and all the promised sweetness of life with her half-planned, when something came to pass abruptly that threw his will and all his little calculations into a dark chaos of amazement where, by a kind of electrically swift reaction, he realized that the one true, possible and right thing for him was this very love he was about to cast aside. His highest destiny was upon the unchanged old earth... with Miriam... and Winky...

She turned and flung her arms round his neck in a passion of tears as though she had divined his unspoken temptation... and at the same time this awful new thing was upon them both. It caught them like a tempest. For a disharmony—a discord—a lying sound was loose upon the air from those two voices far below.

"Call me by my true name," she cried quickly, in an anguish of terror; "for my soul is afraid... Oh, love me most utterly, utterly, utterly... and save me!"

Unnerved and shaking like a leaf, Spinrobin pressed her against his heart.

"I know you by name and you are mine," he tried to say, but the words never left his lips. It was the love surging up in his tortured heart that alone held him to sanity and prevented—as it seemed to him in that appalling moment—the dissolution of his very being and hers.

For Philip Skale had somewhere *uttered falsely*.

A darting zigzag crack, as of lightning, ran over the giant fabric of vibrations that covered the altering world as with a flood... and sounds that no man may hear and not die leaped awfully into being. The suddenness and immensity of the catastrophe blinded these two listening children-souls. Awe and terror usurped all other feelings... but one. Their love, being born of the spirit, held supreme, insulating them, so to speak, from all invading disasters.

Philip Skale had made a mistake in the pronunciation of the Name.

The results were dreadful and immediate, and from all the surface of the wakening world rose anguished voices. Spinrobin started up, lifting Miriam into his arms. He spun dizzily for a moment between boulders and trees, giving out a great wailing cry, unearthly enough had there been any to hear it. Then he began to run wildly through the thick darkness. In his ear—for her head lay close—he heard her dear voice, between the sobs of collapse, calling his inner name most sweetly; and the sound summoned to the front all in him that was best and manly.

"My sweet Master, my sweet Master!"

But he did not run far. About him on every side the night lifted as though it were suddenly day. He saw the summits of the bleak mountains agleam with the reflection of some great light that rushed upon them from the valley. All the desolate landscape, hesitating like some hovering ocean between the old pattern and the new, seemed to hang suspended amid the desolation of the winter skies. Everything roared. It seemed the ground shook. The very bones of the woods went shuddering together; the hills toppled; and overhead, in some incredible depths of space, boomed sounds as though the heavens split off into fragments and hurled the constellations about the vault to swell these shattering thunders of a collapsing world.

The Letters of that terrible and august Name were passing over the face of the universe—distorted because mispronounced—creative sounds, dishevelled and monstrous, because incompletely and incorrectly uttered.

"Put me down," he heard Miriam cry where she lay smothered in his arms, "and we can face everything together, and be safe. Our love is bigger than it all and will protect us..."

"Because it is complete," he cried incoherently in reply, seizing the truth of her thought, and setting her upon the ground; "it includes even this. It is a part of... the Name... correctly uttered... for it is true and pure."

He heard her calling his inner name, and he began forthwith to call her own as they stood there clinging to one another, mingling arms and hair and lips in such a tumult of passion that it seemed as though all this outer convulsion of the world was a small matter compared to the commotion in their own hearts, revolutionized by the influx of a divine love that sought to melt them into a single being.

And as they looked down into the valley at their feet, too bewildered to resist these mighty forces that stole the breath from their throats and the strength from their muscles, they saw with a clearness as of day that the House of Awe in which their love had wakened and matured was passing away and being utterly consumed.

In a flame of white fire, tongued and sheeted, streaked with gulfs of black, and most terribly roaring, it rose with a prodigious crackling of walls and roof towards the sky. Volumes of coloured smoke, like hills moving, went with it; and with it, too, went the forms—the substance of their forms, at least, of their "sounds" released—of Philip Skale, Mrs. Mawle, and all the paraphernalia of gongs, drapery, wires, sheeted walls, sand-patterns, and the preparations of a quarter of a century of labour and audacious research. For nothing could possibly survive in such a furnace. The heat of it struck their faces where they stood even here high upon the hills, and the currents of rising wind blew the girl's tresses across his eyes and moved his own feathery hair upon his head. The notes of those leaping flames were like thunder.

"Watch now!" cried Miriam, though he divined the meaning from the gesture of her free hand rather than actually heard the words.

And, leaning their trembling bodies against a great boulder behind them, they then saw in the midst of the conflagration, or hovering dimly above it rather, the vast outlines of the captured sounds—the Letters—escaping back again into the womb of eternal silence from which they had been with such appalling courage evoked. In forms of dazzling blackness they passed upwards in their chariots of flame, yet at the same time passed *inwards* in some amazing kind of spiral motion upon their own axes, vanishing away with incredible swiftness and beauty deep down into themselves... and were gone.

Realizing in some long-forgotten fashion of childhood the fearful majesty of the wrath of Jehovah, yet secretly undismayed because each felt so gloriously lost in their wonderful love, the bodies of Miriam and Spinrobin dropped instinctively upon their knees, and, still tightly clasped in one another's arms, bowed their foreheads to the ground, touching the earth and leaves.

But how long they rested thus upon the heart of the old earth, or whether they slept, or whether, possibly, the inevitable reaction to all the overstrain of the past hours led them through a period of unconsciousness, neither of them quite knew. Nor was it possible for them to have known, perhaps, that the lonely valley sheltering the House of Awe, running tongue-like into these desolate hills, had the unenviable reputation of trembling a little in sympathy with any considerable shock of earthquake that came to move that portion of the round globe from her sleep. Of this they knew as little, no doubt, as they did of the ill-defined line of demarcation between experiences that are objective, capable of being weighed and measured, and those that are subjective, taking place—though with convincing authority—only in the sphere of the mind...

All they do know, and Spinrobin tells it with an expression of supreme happiness upon his shining round face, is that at length they stirred as they lay, opened their eyes, turned and looked at one another, then stood up. On Miriam's hair and lashes lay the message of the dew, and in her clear eyes all the soft beauty of the stars that had watched over them.

But the stars themselves had gone. Over the hills ran the coloured feet of the dawn, swift and rosy, touching the spread of heathery miles with the tints of approaching sunrise. The tops of the leafless trees stirred gently with a whisper of wind that stole up from the distant sea. The birds were singing. Over the surface of the old earth flew the magical thrill of life. It caught these two children-lovers, sweeping them into each other's arms as with wings.

Out of all the amazing tempest of their recent experiences emerged this ever-growing splendour of their deep and simple love. The kindly earth they had chosen beckoned them down into the valley; the awful heaven they had rejected smiled upon them approvingly, as the old sun topped the hills and peeped upon them with his glorious eye.

"Come, Miriam," breathed Spinrobin softly into her little ear; "we'll go down into another valley... and live happily together forever and ever..."

"Yes," she murmured, blushing with the rosiness of that exquisite winter's dawn; "... you and I... and... and..."

But Spinrobin kissed the unborn name from her lips. "Hush!" he whispered, "hush!"

For the little "word" between these two was not yet made flesh. But the dawn-wind caught up that "hush" and carried it to the trees and undergrowth about them, and then ran thousand-footed before them to whisper it to the valley where they were going.

And Miriam, knowing the worship and protection in his delicate caress, looked up into his face and smiled—and the smile in her grey eyes was that ancient mother-smile which is coeval with life. For the word of creation flamed in these two hearts, waiting only to be uttered.

For more Tales of the Weird titles
visit the British Library Shop (shop.bl.uk)

We welcome any suggestions, corrections or feedback you may have,
and will aim to respond to all items addressed to the following:

The Editor (Tales of the Weird), British Library Publishing,
The British Library, 96 Euston Road, London NW1 2DB

We also welcome enquiries through our Twitter account, @BL_Publishing.